No Regrets,
No Remorse

Books by R.F. Sharp

No Regrets, No Remorse

No Regrets,
No Remorse

A Sydney Simone Mystery

R.F. Sharp

Poisoned Pen Press

Poisoned Pen Press
6962 E. First Ave., Ste. 103
Scottsdale, AZ 85251
www.poisonedpenpress.com
info@poisonedpenpress.com

Printed in the United States of America

To the one true artist, Susannah

Acknowledgments

I am grateful to all the literary agents, especially Grace Morgan, who wisely rejected my early manuscripts, forcing me to rewrite, revise, chop, and reassemble the story until it came together. Thank you Elise Troczynski and Tarah Ash for your support and advice and especially Christine Crilly, my first reader and biggest fan. The people at Poisoned Pen are terrific and helped shape the final version of this story, leaving seeds for the next.

Chapter One

The job was just outside Ann Arbor, Michigan, and though Sydney could have flown directly to Detroit Metro, she took the safer route, a crowded Delta flight to Louisville that would return the next evening. The lie she fed Oscar was a Manhattan shopping trip. Avoiding the slightest risk plus adding a little deception had kept her alive thus far, and she seemed to get more rather than less cautious as time went on. After renting a car using an alternate driving license, she checked into the airport Holiday Inn Express, retrieved the package she had sent ahead, got some fast food to eat on the way, then drove the six hours to Ann Arbor. It was mid-November; cold and overcast, already getting dark. Perfect timing and perfect weather. The drive wasn't bad, and Sydney used the time to think, not listening to the radio.

Just off I-94 about thirty miles from Ann Arbor, the local Walmart had the weapons she needed. The hardware section yielded a small sledge hammer, wire cutters, gloves, various screwdrivers, a small socket set, flashlight, adjustable wrench, and a canvas tool bag. After paying cash, everything but the flashlight and the screwdrivers went into the trunk.

Walmart had security cameras trained on the parking lot, so she traveled side roads seeking a spot with more privacy where she could commit the first crime of the trip. The best choice was a small Greek restaurant with no lights in the lot behind the building. The parked cars in back were probably those of employees and would likely stay until closing. Thin snow slicked the grass, but the pavement was cleared and dry, so no tracks to worry about.

Working quickly, she removed the license plate from a Honda and put it on a Ford that looked similar to her rental. The Ford plate she put on the rental, and the rental plate went in the trunk. Then a half hour more to Ann Arbor.

Mason Feuher lived in an exclusive neighborhood near the Huron River northwest of town. The lots were three to five heavily wooded acres, the winding paved asphalt roads threading through an eighteen-hole golf course. Unlike Florida, there were few gated communities here, even in the affluent areas, which made the job easier. Mason's house was not visible from the road. It was that hateful style she called "Garage Door Architecture": a colonial two-story, its primary feature being a huge two-car garage door, painted white to make a statement—look at me.

From Sydney's extensive research and from the information provided by the client, she knew that Mason would not be home from work until after seven. Mason's office was a forty-five-minute drive even if he didn't stop for his usual drink. To be sure there was time to make all the preparations and set the trap, she called his office from the burn phone and hung up when put through by his secretary. He was some sort of financial planner but enjoyed rather nasty hobbies involving children when not working. Lived alone. No dog.

The telephone line and utilities were underground. A careful walk around the house, checking the windows with the flashlight, looking for but not finding alarm sensors or security cameras. The utilities entered the basement wall near the gas meter. Very convenient, since it allowed her to open the telephone access box and unplug the two lines that fed the house. She then drove around the area for twenty minutes, passing the driveway from time to time. No security or police showed. It was safe to assume Mason didn't have a hard-wired monitored alarm system, since it would have been set off with the disconnect of the telephone line.

The newest thing—and a challenge for those in her profession, was the wireless alarm hooked up to a cell phone system with battery backup, perimeter alarms on doors and windows, and motion detectors. Very difficult, but not impossible, to bypass. She suspected this was what he had but was prepared for that too. From the box she had sent to the hotel she pulled out two devices. The first was a cell phone jammer. Not much bigger than a cell phone, it was highly illegal but readily available on the Internet if you had the cash. She powered it up, got some readouts to be sure it was functioning, and turned on the jammer. Simply put, it interfered with cell phone signals within about a one-hundred-foot radius, so no incoming or outgoing calls could be made. The alarm system, if there was one, would now be neutralized. Sydney had taken it with her to the Gardens Mall food court in West Palm and tried it out. The chattering of dozens of bewildered teenagers suddenly cut off from their texting was proof it worked.

Confident now, she pulled back into the driveway and used the second device. It looked like a simple garage door opener, but an older model no longer available. Taped to the outside was a small Allen wrench, which she removed and inserted in a small hole in the base of the opener, then pressed the open button while slowly turning the wrench. The garage door began opening and she pulled the wrench out of the slot, the programming complete. This particular opener had been marketed years ago by a company intending it as a replacement for the one a person lost. Turning the wrench dialed it through all the frequencies until it hit the one for the garage door. It didn't take long for people like Sydney to figure out it could be used on anyone's door, so it was recalled and discontinued. She still had her sources, though.

If Mason had a newer model opener, this wouldn't work, but she had the tools in the trunk and could then have used a heavy screwdriver to pry the sliding glass door off its track on the rear patio. She could also have picked the lock or broken a window but needed to get this done quickly and unobtrusively. No one would know she had been there if this was done right. She drove into the garage, closed the door with the new opener and carried her tool bag into the house. The garage to house door was unlocked—typical. Sure enough, a control box for the alarm system was near the door and beeping loudly. But the house was isolated and it was unlikely neighbors would hear anything. It was possible the alarm would be triggered once the cell jammer was out of range when she left, but if the sheriff showed up it would register as a false alarm with no visible signs of entry.

The basement door was just off the entryway. She pulled out the flashlight. The natural gas furnace was an older model, not one of the newer high-efficiency units, but the sheet metal covers came off easily to expose the innards. It took several hard blows with the sledgehammer, but the rusted cast-iron heat exchanger finally cracked. She made sure the hammer blows were not obvious and the wide crack was visible. It would, when the furnace was running, leak the combusted gas fumes into the forced air ducts throughout the house, filling it with odorless carbon monoxide.

Everything went back together, and before leaving she turned up the heat a few degrees. If the furnace had been newer she would have pulled the flue apart on the gas water heater for the same result, though it might take longer to fill the house with the fumes. She looked for and found a carbon monoxide alarm in the upstairs hallway and reversed the batteries, wiping the fingerprints.

Mason would die in his sleep. Carbon monoxide poisoning due to a faulty furnace was a reasonable cause of death, easily discovered in an autopsy, and would not bring on the extensive investigation that shooting the guy would require. Her experience was that unless it was a high profile case, underfunded and overworked police departments were happy to accept the first reasonable explanation for a death and didn't often dig deep. It would have been simpler for her to wait until Mason was home, ring the doorbell, and shoot him in the head when he answered, but the risk was greater. And the investigation would be dangerous.

After plugging the telephone lines back in and doing a final check to be sure everything was the same as she had found it, except for the furnace, she drove out of the garage and pushed the button on her new remote control. Then back to Louisville to the car rental counter after putting the rental plate back on and dumping the tools. It was too risky to return the other license plate so she tossed it as well and smashed the cell phone, cell jammer, and door opener, though they were probably untraceable. Exhausted, Sydney went to the hotel room for a few hours sleep before the flight home.

Killing the Ann Arbor guy was satisfying. A job well done. Her history showed no patience with child molesters. No regrets, no remorse. It had always been that way.

Chapter Two

Sydney was nude when the telephone rang.

"I'm answering the phone this time." She hopped off the stool and was already reaching for something to put on.

"No. Let it ring. I want to get this sculpture done. Do you need another break?"

"It might be a client." She grabbed her robe as she walked to the wall phone, careful where she stepped in her bare feet on the cluttered concrete floor of the studio. She had removed her piercings and makeup for the session and in her robe looked as if she had just stepped out of the shower.

"That's what I'm afraid of."

Oscar Leopold put the modeling tools on the stand next to the sculpture and wiped the red clay from his hands onto his jeans.

"For God's sake, put on the smock I gave you for your birthday instead of ruining your clothes."

"Next time. You're acting like a wife. Or mother."

Jesse, Oscar's blond Labrador retriever, lay in the corner of the studio, his head between his paws, staring at him. His tail wagged tentatively whenever Oscar looked his way, hoping for a walk.

It was the third call in the last two hours, and Oscar had managed to convince Sydney to ignore them all until now.

"You can't keep a wife. And your mortgage payment is due, Jesse needs to go to the vet, there's the telephone bill and the electric, and," she said as she reached toward the receiver, "you could use a new car." She looked over her shoulder at him, and he nodded reluctantly. Sweeping her straight black hair back, she spoke in her professional voice.

"Attorney Oscar Leopold's office. May I help you?"

Oscar covered the sculpture with a plastic dry cleaner's bag to keep it from drying out while Sydney dealt with the business. The sculpture was a one-fourth scale seated nude he was doing in terra-cotta. After the sculpture was completed, hollowed, and had dried properly, he would fire it in the kiln in the back room, then patina the surface and put it on display in the gallery window. One or two small sculptures a month sold that way, mostly to the tourists who passed by on their way to the more prestigious galleries on Worth Avenue over on the island in Palm Beach. Sometimes a client would commission a bronze, and that would pay the office expenses for a couple of months. A meager existence, but at least he was doing what he wanted. Sydney offered financial help that Oscar refused, wondering at the time where she would get the money, but he'd accepted her offer to work for free as his model, gallery manager, and former girlfriend. For her part it was a low-profile way to live off the radar, ensuring her real business was kept secret, even from Oscar.

Sydney was talking quietly to whoever was on the telephone and taking notes with a piece of charcoal on a sketchpad.

He mouthed silently, 'Is it my mother?' Sydney shook her head.

He had missed his weekly call up to Grosse Pointe where she shared a condo with her third husband. Oscar made at least two trips a year north to see her which was the most he could handle. His brother Gary lived in Lansing, about an hour away, but rarely called or visited, as their mother made a point of mentioning during every call. Who will take care of me when I get old, she often asked, as if she were assuming it would not be her husband or Gary.

Oscar was washing the remaining red clay from his hands in the corner sink when Sydney held the telephone out to him.

"It's Roy. He's calling from jail. He's been arrested for murder."

He took the call, spoke briefly, then hung up.

"Get dressed. It's time to play lawyer. We're going to jail."

Chapter Three

Oscar showered and put on his lawyer's uniform: dark suit, white shirt, tie, black loafers. He still owned six tailor-made suits. They were getting a little shiny in the seat and elbows and Oscar had no idea whether the lapel width and cut was currently in style. He hadn't been in a good clothing store in the five years since he'd quit full-time practice. They still fit, though they were beginning to get a little tight in the waist, a situation he liked to think meant the suits had somehow shrunk from lack of use. Sydney was no help in the fashion department, preferring that he dress in all black Armani, including the shirt and, if he insisted, a tie. Not suitable lawyer attire according to the ultra conservative judges in the area.

He smoothed down his short blond hair with his palms, no combing necessary now that he had given up his ponytail, admitted that he was balding, and had what was left cropped close to the scalp.

Sydney came into the room in all black minus the piercings and the Goth eye shadow, remnants, she said, of her forlorn and unconventional high school days that she wasn't ready to abandon. It was the way she rolled, as she put it.

"Ready?" she asked.

"I should shave."

"I don't think you need to shave to go to jail. It's pretty informal." They went down the back stairs.

"I hope the Toyota starts," he said.

"Not likely. Do you know how old it is in human years? Ninety-six."

"How do you figure? You using dog years?"

"Same deal except cars are eight years instead of seven." She opened the door to the Toyota and cranked it over until the battery wore down.

"Let's try the Buick. It's a hundred and four, but usually reliable." Oscar stepped over to the rusting black and white four door, clearly a former police car. It was covered with rotting tangerines and leaves from the tree he had parked under three weeks earlier. He opened the door and let it air out a bit before getting in. The built-up heat in the closed car carried the smell of old cigarettes and an unidentifiable perfume. The motor turned over reluctantly, but didn't start.

Pumping the gas pedal, then holding it to the floor and turning the key again caused the beast to rumble to life, belching blue smoke, mostly out the hole in the muffler rather than the exhaust pipe. Rolling down the windows, he backed out into the alley. Sydney got in and they left for the county jail, trailing tangerines, leaves, and branches.

"Why can't we take the Mustang? This thing stinks and it's hot." Sydney had her head out the window, hair flying.

"The Mustang doesn't have air conditioning either; it's a '65. A classic. You know I only drive it on special occasions."

The traffic was, as usual for February, thick and slow moving. From December to April the streets were crowded, the restaurants required a wait at any time of day, and prices escalated on everything from a round of golf to the cost of bait at the marina. Having grown up in the North, Oscar forgave it all as the price of being free of snow.

They pulled into the parking lot of the Main Detention Center, the largest of the four jails in the county, holding up to 1500 inmates. There were no parking spaces left near the entrance except one reserved for Official Vehicles Only. Oscar jerked the aging Buick into the spot.

Sydney looked at him but said nothing.

"Hey, I'm as official as any of them. Besides, the car probably feels right at home since it probably worked here at one time. It still has the holes in the roof where the police strobe light bar was removed."

"I know, it leaks in the rain, even through your duct tape repair. I'll wait in the car in case we have to move it."

"No, you're my legal assistant now, call it a promotion. There's a briefcase in the back with paper and pens. You can help me with the interview. Besides, Roy likes you and needs all the moral support he can get."

"I don't suppose the promotion comes with pay."

They both got out of the car. Sydney looked around anxiously at the uniformed police walking into and out of the facility. There were a half dozen patrol cars in the lot. This was not the kind of place where she liked to hang out.

The intense heat disappeared when they stepped into the air conditioning of the jail's lobby. The waiting room was crowded with visitors, mostly women and children, talking quietly until they could see their incarcerated family members. Two small Latino girls, about three and five, played on the tile floor with a plastic pail and shovels intended for beach and sand.

"I wonder what will be their future," Sydney said softly. "Will the memories of visiting Daddy in jail follow them?"

After showing ID they passed through a security checkpoint and metal detector, signed in with the desk officer, went downstairs, and waited in a small windowless room for them to bring Roy. It was about eight feet square and furnished with a green Formica-topped gray steel table and two straight-backed chairs, all bolted to the floor. The fluorescent ceiling lights were turned on from the wall switch outside the room.

"The smell of urine gives the space just the right atmosphere for the situation, doesn't it?" Sydney started to sit in one of the chairs, changed her mind, and leaned against the wall.

There was one knock on the door and a middle-aged deputy immediately opened it, admitting Roy, who looked out of character without his three-piece suit, wearing instead the too-small beltless jumpsuit and shoestring-less wingtips.

"You have five minutes with your lawyer." The deputy closed the door and stood outside.

"What happened to your shoestrings?" said Oscar.

"They took them away so I wouldn't hang myself—as if a shoestring could support my weight. Oscar. Sydney. Thank God you're here. Did you arrange an early arraignment and bail yet?"

"We just got here." Oscar stood and extended his hand. Roy grabbed it with both of his own and shook it vigorously after Oscar evaded his attempt to hug him.

"Oscar's not a hugger." Sydney stayed pressed against the wall. "Unless you're a good-looking female."

"Got a cigarette?"

"You don't smoke. Plus, they don't allow smoking in here anymore." Oscar said.

"I think I'm going to start."

"So what's this all about, Roy? What have they got on you?" Oscar sat down in one of the chairs.

Sydney pulled a ball point pen and legal pad from the briefcase, and still standing, got ready to take notes. She whispered, "Is the room bugged? Should we write instead of talk?"

"No. Lawyers and clients have the right to interview in private." Roy said, his round face streaming with sweat despite the air conditioning. He looked quickly all over the room, though the only thing to see was the two of them.

"I don't know all the details. I thought Big Jack's death was an accident. His boat exploded with him in it and also killed a passerby. In fact, I was planning to represent his wife in a wrongful death case. Do you remember Lucy? And I was checking into who contaminated the fuel, looking toward filing suit when the cops moved in. I guess the lawsuit's out the window now."

"Wait a minute," Sydney said, "You mean Big Jack Burdine, the guy who advertises on television and billboards? The one where he's standing on his head with the caption, 'I'll stand on my head to get you justice'—that Jack?"

"Yes. I thought you knew I was working for him now."

"No. I didn't," Sydney said.

"I did," Oscar said. "So what did you mean the police moved in?"

"The detectives. They had to interview everyone in depth. They were real interested in the materials in Jack's office. You know what a mess that was. I couldn't get anything out of them but the implication was that his death was a possible homicide."

Oscar leaned back in the chair. Sydney had yet to take a note. "I was in his office once. Good luck with searching that. The piles of files on the floor and desk were so high I could only see him from the chin up. He said he had a system worked out with Lucy, that he could put his finger on anything, anytime. I doubted it. So what happened?"

"They stayed for a few days talking to everyone and were trying to get a court order for the office records. We stopped them from taking any client files at first on the attorney-client confidentiality basis, but we're still fighting the State's Attorney.

"Then today they came back. I've never even seen these detectives before, and they arrested me. Right in the office in front of the staff. Took me out in fucking handcuffs! I could only get a little information out of them."

"Why do they think Jack was murdered and that you did it?"

"From what they told me the boat's fuel line was cut. Gasoline had been added to the diesel fuel to make it more explosive. Some kind of igniter was used. They say it was no accident and can ascribe motive, means, and opportunity to me." Roy wiped his palm across his face from forehead to chin, a habit Oscar had always found particularly annoying, then stood and paced in the tiny space behind the table.

"They say we argued, he struck me, I threatened him, and stood to take over the business with him gone."

"Is that true?"

"Sure, but that's not a case. Hell, it's entirely circumstantial."

"Circumstantial is enough for a death sentence sometimes." Oscar said.

"I know. Thanks for being so positive. But I have an alibi. They either haven't checked it out or don't believe it. Besides, you know I'd never kill anybody no matter what I said."

"Tell me about the alibi."

"I was with Lucy when Jack died. I had been seeing her off and on. Jack didn't know. We were working late in the office on a case. You talk to her. She'll vouch for me." He sat down and leaned back, his big belly nearly splitting the cheap fabric of the jumpsuit.

"Did you tell the police about this?"

"Of course, but I don't know what the problem is. Maybe they haven't been able to talk to her. She might be hiding out to avoid the press." He frowned.

"Oscar, you know I couldn't kill Jack or anybody else. He had plenty of trouble and lots of other people who hated him, believe me. But I'm the least likely candidate for murderer. Talk to Lucy. She'll tell you." He reached across the table, grabbing Oscar's hand.

"Let me get this straight," said Sydney, "you were screwing Lucy, Jack's wife. You got in an argument. He hit you. You threatened him. You stand to take over the law practice. Sounds like a lot of motive to me. I mean this is just from watching *Law and Order* reruns, but still."

Jack stared at her, then turned to Oscar.

"Oscar, I want you to defend me."

Oscar blinked twice.

"Before you say anything, listen." He let go of Oscar's hand and folded both arms on the table top. "I know you haven't done much trial work lately, and I know I can get all the lawyers I want somewhere else. Criminal law specialists. But I want you. We started out together. Through law school, moving here from Detroit, taking the bar exam, we've been through it all. We should still be partners if you hadn't decided to become an art bum." He grinned. "I know you'll take a personal interest in my case. I know you're good and won't compromise me. I'm asking this as a friend. If you never do anything else for me, please do this."

Oscar looked him in the eyes and hesitated for a few seconds. The hum of the air conditioning duct overhead was the only sound in the room. He turned and looked at Sydney. She nodded slightly and looked at the floor.

"I tell you what I can do. I can represent you through the arraignment. Let me see if I can get you out of here. They may go for bail depending on how they charge you."

"No. I want you full-time and all the way through, no matter what."

"This is a capital offense. Could be death penalty stuff if they ask for it." Oscar said quietly.

"You think I don't know that? I want you."

Oscar closed his eyes, took a deep breath, exhaled slowly. "Okay I'll take the case."

"Great," Roy smiled, put his hands flat on the table and leaned forward. "Now listen. I'm going to write you a check for a retainer. And don't tell me you're doing this as a freebee. I want this on a professional level so if you screw up I can sue for malpractice." He smiled slightly. "If we go to trial I'll get you some more."

"Very funny. Okay. We can talk about the fee later. I'll talk to Lucy and do some checking around. Right now we'll see if we can get the judge to give you a Saturday arraignment so we can possibly get bond set and get you out of here before Monday. This is a capital crime so bail is going to be through the roof if they allow it at all. What you have going for you is no record and the fact you're a member of the bar. I hope you contributed to the judge's re-election fund."

"I always give money to anyone who wants to run for judge. You never know when it might come back to help you."

Oscar stood and knocked on the door, signaling the guard.

"Don't go anywhere. I'll be in touch."

"Right. You're not funny either."

Oscar and Sydney signed out and headed down the steps to the Buick, which amazingly had been neither towed nor ticketed.

Chapter Four

"Oh good. Customers," Sydney scanned the new messages on her encrypted email account. The emails all originated from her website, HumanPestControl.com, which had been registered though an offshore intermediary in the Dominican Republic. Impossible for the Whois database of domain names to trace it back to her. This had been very important in keeping her out of jail—and alive—thus far.

The first was a call for help for a sexual harassment problem from a young woman who could not afford to lose her job by filing a complaint with the authorities. Being in the country illegally closed a lot of doors for her, so she was desperate. Sydney had handled a few of these before and saved the request to another file for investigation later. If the complaint was legitimate and the client could afford the fee, she would likely take the case. But first she would determine how much trouble it might be before giving the woman a quote.

Her room was on the ground floor of Oscar's building, at the back behind the gallery and his studio, under the second floor loft apartment. She had secured her room by installing a steel door and door frame. The walls were concrete block, as was the building, so security was good. Oscar thought he had a key, but the one Sydney had given him didn't work, though he had never complained so she assumed he had never tried to use it. While a casual observer might not notice anything unusual outside the assault rifle on a rack over the desk, this was the operations center for her real business. Between missions she helped Oscar run the Rose Madder Gallery up front. He was unaware of her true vocation.

The business was advertised online as a problem solving service. She maintained Youtube and Facebook sites under an assumed name. Customers came to her after exhausting all other remedies. After the police and the lawyers failed, after reasoning, complaining and self-help didn't solve the problem, contact Human Pest Control.

The deal was half the money down and half on completion. No refunds for failure and no guarantee of success. She had learned about collections. The rule of the prostitute was her financial guide. That is, the perceived value of the service diminished significantly once the service was performed. She made it clear that if the job was a success and the second half was not paid, the client then became the victim. Sydney had no accounts receivable.

Sydney folded her laptop closed, locked up, went out back and started her Harley to go down to the mail drop. It was a half-hour from West Palm, depending on the traffic. Sydney hadn't been down there in ten days or so.

She was expecting the second payment from the completed Ann Arbor job and didn't like to leave unattended cash. The Pack and Ship store where she forwarded her mail had always been safe enough, but she trusted no one. The street around the store had no parked cars and there was only one customer to wait out before she entered the store. The private mailboxes were to the left of the sales counter and she kept her helmet on when she went inside, nodding to the owner, Paul, whom she had seen before. There were several letters and one package about the size of a box of checks in the box. No one was in the letter box area of the store so she opened it.

Hundred-dollar bills. Five packs of ten thousand each, wrapped in paper bands and a note. The note had a code number she provided to cases she was taking and the words, 'Do it soon'.

This could be a problem. The second half she was expecting was only supposed to be ten thousand, and the coded number didn't match the case. What was this? Then she realized it had to be the Big Jack Gamble client. Gamble was the guy Roy was accused of murdering.

One technique Sydney used from time to time for cases she really didn't want to take was to quote a price so outrageously high that the client was scared off. Mostly she never heard from them again. This time the guy paid the exorbitant amount anyway. Somebody else did the job before she could set it up. So, a bonus. She had investigated the original request pretty thoroughly to be sure of two things. First that the target deserved to die, and second, that the deal wasn't a setup. Sydney's business—and moral compass—demanded she be certain the information given her was legitimate as well as not from the police.

There were no details in the original email as to the reason for the hit, but it didn't fit her model, so she asked for fifty thousand, thinking that would be the end of it. There was no return address on the envelope so she couldn't return it anyway.

She put the money in the inside jacket pocket and headed home. A nice day's work for doing nothing. She would add the money to her stash. No refunds and no way she knew of that he could find her. A foreign Internet service provider made tracking her impossible. The cash deposits were sent to a mail forwarding service in Manhattan which then sent them on to her private mailbox drop in Pompano Beach. It seemed safe enough, though she had to appear in person to set up the mail drops.

She remembered the email request for a hit on Gamble. She had almost said something when Roy told them he was accused of the murder. Someone else had beat her to it. Could it be Roy? Was this too much a coincidence?

She had to get back to the gallery to set up the new show. Oscar, though a decent artist, had no eye for arranging the paintings on the gallery walls.

Chapter Five

A terrifying note arrived in her inbox the next day. It was from the rejected client who had sent her the fifty thousand. Getting emails complaining about her inaction when she kept the money but didn't do the job was not unusual. When nothing happened the ones she ripped off usually sent numerous pleading or threatening emails. Useless. Then they gave up since she had no physical address they could locate. They couldn't very well go to the police complaining that she wouldn't carry out the killing. It was her way of punishing them for their bad thoughts.

The problem was that this time he referred to her by name, though she never gave that out. Implying he had found her. It seemed impossible. Her security was as tight as she could make it. Was she at risk? And how much more did he know?

Giving the money back wouldn't be a problem, but he specifically stated that a refund was not an option. He knew Big Jack was dead, but also knew she could not have done it, given the timing. Apparently he had sent the money the same day Jack's boat exploded, though she hadn't retrieved the cash until days later.

He demanded a telephone call or meeting. An in-person meeting was of course out of the question. But he knew her name—at least the one she was using now. She didn't think he could find where she lived. All her personal accounts, driver's license, and passport used the mail drop address. So how had he found her? There were ways, but you had to practically be the police or a world-class hacker to access them.

She would use the burn phone now from another location in the event he had technology that could track it. Then deep-six the phone. The best place to make the call would be downtown. A busy place. Maybe from the art museum parking lot. Lots of escape routes.

A rare parking space in the shade was available, and she shut off the bike. The cell was one of the older flip phones that she powered on. The client called himself Rico and had a 561 area code, which was local. Nothing came back on a reverse telephone lookup on the Internet, but then cell phone numbers couldn't be tracked easily that way. Also nothing when she Googled the number, so she was flying blind. Before she could dial the number the telephone rang, startling her. The phone didn't have caller ID. She let it ring three more times, and then pushed the send key to answer it.

"Hello?"

"Rico here. How you doing Sydney?"

A long pause. He must have gotten the name and number from her mail drop. She hoped no one got hurt giving up the information. They had no address for her, so Rico wouldn't have one either.

"Funny name, Rico."

"My father's idea. Racketeering, influence peddling, corruption and organized crime, the RICO statutes. Yeah, he's a riot. A lawyer believe it or not. Anyway, I like it."

"What is it you want? I can give your money back, and the target is gone."

"I paid for a service, and I always get what I pay for. Now it's true the original object of the deal is no longer around, but I have another one that is kind of urgent, so I'm making a substitution."

"It doesn't work that way. You send me the details, I check it out, then decide if I want the job."

"Too late for that. I paid, you took the money. You get the other half when the job's done. Understand that I want to keep this professional, but if I have to I'll ensure your cooperation."

"If you have such resources why don't you just do the job yourself?"

"I hire people to work for me. I don't do my own plumbing, either. So I hired you and you will do the job, or you and people you know will be the next contract."

"Send me the info and I'll think on it." Sydney disconnected, climbed on her bike, then sat there. She had no friends except Oscar. The people she knew were mostly those who worked the neighborhood restaurants and her mechanic, not friends. The obvious solution would be to track down Rico and eliminate him if she could. Or disappear. She had plenty of cash and could start over in a new location. But there was Oscar. Not love exactly, but he was her only real connection to the human race.

She tossed the phone in the Intracoastal on the way home.

Chapter Six

It was nearly five o'clock. The Friday-go-home-from-work traffic and the let's-go-out-for-dinner-with-the-other-retirees-for-the-early-bird-special crowd combined to constipate the main roads. Oscar pulled into a 7-Eleven to use the pay phone to call Big Jack's wife, Lucy. When he remembered to bring his cell phone with him, typically he'd forgotten to put it on the charger. She had already left the office, but the receptionist said she would call Lucy's beeper for him, so he headed back to the gallery to wait. He planned to pin down the alibi defense and get Roy quickly off the hook.

She called an hour after he got back. He was two glasses into a bottle of Sydney's Cabernet and had smoked a half pack of cigarettes by then, sitting on his balcony overlooking the street, the cell phone beside him. This was his third pack of cigarettes of the day, though he had only smoked two or three from the first two packs before tossing the rest in the trash. It was his way of trying to quit, an expensive method what with the increasing per-pack cost. He never bought a carton, rationalizing that if he only bought one pack at a time he wasn't actually addicted.

The shops were closing across from him, and the sun was setting over the rooftops. He had always meant to live within view of the ocean when he moved to Florida, but never seemed to find the right place. He remembered when his mother had brought him to Florida as a child and he had seen the ocean for the first time. It seemed like a vast blue wall stretching high above and left and right, threatening to come pouring down upon him. That hooked him for life. He got the ocean breeze up on the balcony when the wind was right, a plus.

"Oscar. It's me. I assume this is about Roy."

Oscar knew who "me" was since he was expecting her call, but wouldn't otherwise have recognized Lucy's voice. They had met only twice, briefly at opening receptions for artists at the gallery, the last time almost a year ago. He had no feelings about her, neither like nor dislike. He could visualize her, though. Tall and thin with thick, long, red hair, and a certain hardness around her eyes caused maybe from too much sun and her forty-something or maybe from some harsh early years. She had those painted-on eyebrows that some women preferred, more an artificial than a natural look. Sydney said they were tattooed on, which Oscar found bizarre. He did remember her eyes, though. They were Elizabeth Taylor eyes, that violet color, the one feature most people remembered about her.

They arranged to meet for dinner at the Ebb Tide, a seafood restaurant and bar on the edge of the Intracoastal Waterway near Lantana. The open-air lounge side faced the water, and fishing boats from the small marina next door would cruise by just beyond the tables. Very popular with the tourists.

He was interested in seeing how she looked as a grieving widow. She hadn't sounded too distraught over the telephone. In honor of the fact that he was taking a good-looking woman to dinner, Oscar shaved and kept his tie on. Looking in the bathroom mirror he decided his suit wasn't too badly wrinkled to be worn. The restaurant was likely to be dimly lit. The Buick graciously started, and he met Lucy in the lobby on time.

She gave Oscar a little cheek-peck, a quick but distant hug whether he liked it or not, then they took a table on the patio near the water. She had dressed for the occasion and wore a tight, black, above the knees and below the armpits dress with a side dish of diamond earrings. She smelled of perfume he recognized mixed with the stale whiff of cigarette smoke.

Cheesy little plastic Japanese lanterns and fake string fishnets were strung along the beams of the pergola overhead to give the place an affected seaside ambience. Oscar ordered a mid-range California Merlot and watched Lucy light a cigarette. He would have lit it for her but thought she might be offended by the offer, not being familiar with her philosophy of male-female role expectations. He lit one of his own. The woman at the table behind Lucy turned to look and coughed at them. They were in an outdoor area so technically they could smoke, but it was getting harder to find a place. There were no signs, but no ashtrays either. Lucy stared glassy eyed out at the water for a moment before she spoke. Oscar thought she was doing a pretty good widow so far.

"I've been trying not to drink so much, but since Jack's death it's been difficult."

"Wine with dinner doesn't count," Oscar replied. He was aware that the elderly, obviously tourist couple behind Lucy could hear their conversation. The woman was motioning for the waiter.

"You were married weren't you Oscar? And there was a child?"

"Yes. We divorced." He hoped she didn't press the child issue. The death of Oscar's son Tad had been the insidious catalyst to the breakdown of both Oscar's psyche and his marriage. He never talked about it, refused to even if anyone else tried to broach the subject in an effort at offering him solace. He had spent a few months in a private psychiatric hospital, but would never talk about that either. That was when he took up smoking, something he'd never done before.

"Was it awful?" she asked.

"At the time it was. She thought I was crazy, even tried to have me committed."

Lucy's eyes widened.

"Didn't work, though. I gave up the practice. Gave it to Roy. He and I went to law school together in Detroit. After graduation, we moved to Florida, got an apartment, and worked at odd jobs while we studied for the bar exam. Roy worked as a shoe salesman, and I waited tables at Denny's. We passed the exam at first taking, and both landed jobs with the Florida Public Defender's Office.

"After three years of helping shoplifters continue to shop, drunk drivers keep driving, and the occasional alleged murderer stay out of jail, we opened our own office, Flagler and Leopold."

"Not Leopold and Flagler?"

"We flipped a coin. Anyway, long story short, the practice grew quickly—too quickly. We were swamped with general practice work. Roy handled most of the civil cases, and I did the divorce and criminal stuff. We both married our secretaries and bought identical houses in the same subdivision in Lake Worth. Roy still lives there, down the street from my ex-wife Pam and her new boyfriend.

"In retrospect, I think the whole problem was burnout from too many divorce cases. I tended to take on people's problems as my own. Too many battered wives and kidnapped children." And, he thought, too much grief.

"Couldn't leave it at the office?" she asked.

"I guess not. Now at thirty-eight, I've been a licensed, if not full-time lawyer, for eleven years and a more or less professional sculptor for five."

"Any chance of remarrying?"

"Never say never."

Lucy blew out a long trail of smoke and squinted at him through the haze. "What about Sydney? I thought you were living with her?"

"No. Nothing going. Just a business relationship. Tell me about you and Jack. I mean, face it, you and Roy were hooking up, so there must have been a problem."

"Not much to tell. Jack and I had each other and not much else. No friends really. Jack wasn't the type to keep friends for very long. You know how he was. You and I haven't been friends, Oscar, but I want to share. I had accepted Jack's death as soon as I heard. His health and lifestyle—a heart attack wouldn't have surprised me. But still it was hard. We went through a lot together. I know people talked about him, and his manners weren't the best. I tried to teach him some social graces. He was not a popular man, but I haven't yet accepted that he could have been murdered. Then Roy and I just started seeing each other." She flicked the accumulating ashes from the cigarette over the rail and into the water. The woman behind her was speaking softly but emphatically into the ear of the waiter.

"And if it was murder, Roy didn't do it." She looked right through Oscar's eyes with her violet ones. "I know they think he had good reason to do it, but he's not violent."

"Roy says he was with you at the office that night."

"Yes. At least until six. I had to leave and pick up a few things on the way home. I usually shop on Tuesdays."

"But the boat exploded just after seven, didn't it?" Oscar had reviewed the newspaper accounts from his I'm-going-to-recycle-these-someday pile at home.

"Seven-sixteen is what the police said."

"So you weren't an alibi then?"

"I am. He was with me and had a lot to do after I left. When I came in on Wednesday the work was done." She tossed her cigarette into the water. A second waiter who had just arrived with the wine looked like he was about to say something but kept his mouth shut. The tip is the thing.

"Not exactly an ironclad alibi, but it is something. So you told the police?" Oscar wondered about her going to work the morning after the death of her husband. This was a cold woman.

"Just this afternoon. On the phone. They want me to come in."

They ordered, she the stone crab and he the prime rib. The waiters were now conferring and their waiter came over and waited politely until he got their attention.

"Excuse me, sir, madam, but this is a nonsmoking establishment."

Oscar looked at him, and keeping eye contact, took one more drag and crushed it out on his bread plate. The waiter smiled and left. Oscar took out his pack, offered it to Lucy, and they both burned fresh ones.

"Was Jack in trouble with anyone you know of? I know this sounds corny, like something on television, but did he have any enemies?"

"Well, no enemies as such. There were a couple of disgruntled clients, ones that had filed complaints with the bar association. But in a high-volume practice like we have—had— there are always some crackpots."

"What kind of complaints?"

"I guess I can tell you, since Jack's gone anyway. There were three. They say Jack settled their cases without their consent and refused to turn over the money. Jack said the cases were worthless, that there was no money coming to them. But the Florida Bar Association is doing an investigation."

"Have any of them threatened him?"

"One of them, a Mr. Cake I think his name is, comes in once in awhile ranting and raving, sometimes breaks stuff. We call the police, and they haul him away. He did it the day of Jack's death. But nothing else. I told the police about him."

Oscar took his little spiral notebook from his jacket breast pocket. He had remembered it this time, and made a note of Cake's name.

"Tell me about the argument Roy and Jack are supposed to have had."

She took a deep drink of wine. He refilled her glass, drank the rest of his, and filled it, too.

"It was earlier in the day. Roy wanted to know when he was going to be made partner. Jack had been stringing him along. I heard part of it when they got a little loud. Jack even slapped him, if you can imagine. He told me he had never had any intention of making Roy a partner, that he didn't need partners."

"Wait a minute. I talked to Roy when he took this job. He told me that Jack had promised a partnership after a year or so in the firm."

"Jack said that to all the associates he hired. He was always careful not to put it in writing and to make the promises a little vague. He once told me people were a lot more motivated when you kept promising to do something for them than if you actually did it. Sort of the reverse of the old axiom, actions speak louder than words."

He thought about the truth of the statement during the meal. That kind of attitude was at best a short-term form of motivation. Oscar contemplated the odd moral values of Big Jack. He was a user, an opportunist who placed his own interests above those of his clients. Oscar thought that he could stand to be just a bit more like that. His ex-wife had told him more than once that they would be a lot richer if he had put his own interests on a par with his clients'.

"What happens to the firm now that Jack is dead?" he asked as the plates were cleared, thinking that maybe he should have said passed away, or passed on.

"I've thought about that, of course. I'm not a lawyer, so even though I'm the wife and sole heir, I can't own anything except the office equipment and the lease on the building. Non-lawyers can't own a law firm. The television ads have been cancelled. Roy is still the senior associate, but he's planning on taking some time off, assuming he gets out of this, and work out of his house to help me out with some things. I suppose the current associates will have to divide the caseload among themselves. Maybe I can work out a deal to sell the equipment and such to them, or get an employment contract as office manager. I don't know. Then there's the Internal Revenue Service and the local tax problems."

He thought they were wrapping up their conversation until he heard that.

"Tell me."

"I thought everybody knew. Big Jack was in deep trouble with the IRS. They were auditing Jack's last three years' returns. Our returns, I should say. He said he might face jail time. They have liens against our condo and were talking about seizing our personal assets. Am I out of all that now that Jack's gone?"

He noted that she had said "gone."

"It depends." He thought about it while he sipped his coffee. Surprisingly she nodded, as if that answer was enough. He had no ashtray, but the Intracoastal was close enough. He lit another. The couple sitting behind Lucy had finished quickly and were now talking to the maître d'.

"What happened to the money? I thought Jack had one of the biggest personal injury practices in the state."

"He did. I was the office manager and Jack's legal assistant. I knew what money came in, but he took care of the money that went out. The investments, he called them. He said he had lost quite a bit in the stock market. I know that's hard to believe a few years ago when everybody else was making a killing, but he liked to invest in those high-risk stock futures. I think that led to the tax trouble. He liked boats, and you know how expensive they are. The Hatteras is hocked to its eyeballs. His fishing boat of course blew up, so I hope the insurance was paid on it. But the thing is, I always had everything I needed, so I didn't ask many questions. But it didn't matter. No matter how much money he made, it wasn't enough. He was always looking for that one big score."

"So you weren't interested in the money?"

"Of course I was. I wanted to live in Palm Beach instead of West Palm with the crime and the scum, but I'm saying we could have had it if he hadn't blown the money on these get-rich-quick deals of his, and his toys."

"Was there any life insurance?" Oscar tried not to be offended by the "scum" reference.

"Yes. But I don't have that yet. They say soon." She wrung her hands, very new-widow-like. Oscar dropped two fifties on the waiter's tray and they stood to go. He smiled at the couple who had been eavesdropping and winked at the woman as they passed, wondering where these people still found matching polyester leisure suits.

A man in a tuxedo stopped them as they were leaving.

"Excuse me sir, but in the future you must refrain from smoking to be welcome here." His obvious hairpiece and too perfect teeth fit right in with what looked like a cheap face-lift. The guy could have been sixty or eighty.

"As far as I'm concerned, wherever I sit is the smoking section, so remember that the next time I come in." Oscar put his cigarette out in the mint bowl near the door. To Lucy he said as he held the door for her, "Blackballed from yet another restaurant."

"I just wonder," Lucy said, "whether Jack could have persuaded Roy to stay if he had lived long enough to have that meeting with him on the boat."

Oscar stopped in the doorway. A young couple stood waiting for him to move out of the way.

"What meeting? What boat?"

"I thought I told you. The night he was killed, Jack had invited Roy to meet at the fishing boat to discuss his complaints. He wanted to keep him around. But," she added quickly, "I don't know for sure that Roy was going to go."

Chapter Seven

The Ebb Tide was located on a side street leading to the west side of the Intracoastal; they called it Lake Worth locally, though technically it was a saltwater lagoon. The area wasn't any more unsafe than anywhere else in West Palm, but the streets could be a bad place to be after dark. At one time the area was in the top ten nationwide for violent crime, a statistic not trumpeted widely by the tourist board. Oscar and Lucy said goodbye with a quick hug and a promise to get in touch in the next day or two and headed for their cars on opposite ends of the lot.

The parking lot was bordered by the marina docks on one side and a small, unlit and overgrown city park on the other. There were thirty or forty cars, vans, SUV's, and pickups scattered under the yellowish outdoor lights. A large white and blue motor home sat parked at the far end. The curtains on the motor home's windows were pulled shut, but the lights were on. Probably someone looking for a cheap campsite in the parking lot. The police would have them moved before too much time passed.

Oscar was trying to coax his car into starting when he heard Lucy scream. He fumbled with the glove compartment, realized it was locked, and quickly found the key to open it and take out the forty-five caliber over-and-under derringer he kept there for emergencies, then hurried out toward the end of the lot where she said she had parked.

There were five hoodlum types standing around her gray BMW. One was at that moment pulling her by the arm out the doorway from behind her steering wheel. Oscar put the hand with the pistol in his right jacket pocket and yelled as he approached.

"Hey! What's going on? Do you guys want to leave the lady alone?"

She stopped screaming then and started sobbing and trying to pull away from the guy holding her arm. He held on. They all turned to Oscar. They were tattooed and dirty, wearing baggy pants, and sideways baseball caps on their heads. Ubiquitous badasses. Gang-bangers. He could see no displayed weapons.

"Fuck you man! Get back in your car and get the fuck out of here unless you want some too," said the guy nearest to Oscar. Oscar was still walking closer, now about three cars away from them.

"We don't want any trouble. I'll give you all my money, my credit cards, everything. Just don't hurt the lady."

"How about if we take the money and everything and the bitch, too?" the same guy said. They all laughed.

"No. Really. Here, take my wallet."

They watched Oscar's hand in the dim light of the parking lot as he pulled out what they thought would be his wallet, but which turned out to be the derringer. He pointed it directly at the groin of the nearest one.

The man he was aiming at was young, maybe twenty, dressed in tan baggie pants and a dark striped T-shirt with the sleeves ripped off. He seemed startled at first, and then his face broke into a wide grin, displaying two empty tooth sockets.

"What you going do with that little thing, you fuck?" He moved forward as if intending to take it. Oscar left it pointed directly at the man's crotch and cocked the hammer back.

"Stop right there and let me tell you about this 'little thing'," Oscar said loudly so that they would all hear. "This is a derringer. Often used by the police as a hideaway backup. It fires two .45 caliber bullets. If I shot you, say, in the knee…" He gestured with it again but not at the man's knee, still aiming at his crotch, and stepped a little closer. The guy stepped back, looking to his friends for support. "You might not die of shock and blood loss if you got to a hospital right away. Of course, you might lose the leg since most of the socket and kneecap would be blown out. If you're lucky, and my aim is off a little you might save it, but forget about playing basketball again or even walking without a limp. And at this distance I just don't see how I could miss." Oscar was sure that his little speech and where he was aiming would make them think and probably back off. He felt a little like Dirty Harry.

He didn't count on the ignorance of the street gang mentality where you act first and think, if at all, much later. The guy lunged for the gun.

In one quick motion Oscar fired, hitting him just as he had threatened in the kneecap before the others realized what was happening. The noise was deafening in the night quiet.

The recoil nearly tore the gun from his hand. Oscar was always amazed that such a small gun could make such a large sound. Lucy pulled loose and ran over behind him, losing one of her high heels in the process. The one banger shot was screaming as he flopped around in a fetal position on his side, holding his leg.

"Jesus Christ, the son-of-a-bitch shot me! Jesus Christ, Jesus Christ! My knee!"

The others were in panic. One jumped over the hood of Lucy's car and ran into the night. Another was digging into his pants pocket, apparently looking for a knife or some other weapon.

"Lie down on the ground, all of you," Oscar yelled as loud and authoritatively as he could, "Put your hands on top of your heads or we're going to have more than one cripple here."

He had seen that line work once in a movie. It worked this time, too. But then he had the gun, and it was pointed at them. The derringer was a two-shot, and he hoped the other barrel was loaded.

"Lucy," he said, trying to pull her off him, "Run back to the restaurant and call the police from there."

"Will you be okay?"

"Get inside the restaurant. Call 911."

She did, fumbling with her purse to get at her cell. He waited, hoping that the three uninjured guys wouldn't try and jump him or that the one who ran off didn't shoot him from the darkness before the police came. He wasn't entirely sure that the derringer would hit what he was aiming at. It was only reliably accurate to about ten feet, and he had gotten lucky with the first shot.

Oscar pointed the gun from one to the other. His knees felt rubbery, and his hand was shaking slightly. He heard a siren nearby, getting louder and hoped it wasn't a fire engine. He wanted a cigarette badly. A police cruiser roared into the parking lot with sirens blowing and lights flashing just after Lucy left and too soon to be responding to her call. He placed the gun on the hood of the car nearest him and put his hands in the air. No sense them thinking he was the bad guy.

The cops were taking no chances. They jumped from their car with guns drawn and aimed directly at him. Oscar strained to get his arms higher just so there would be no misunderstanding.

"This crazy bastard shot me!" yelled the guy on the ground. He was in a ball, holding his knee and writhing, smearing dark blood over the pavement. His pants leg was shiny wet-black in the yellow light. He was getting noticeably paler, probably from shock, Oscar thought. The forty-five really could literally tear off a leg if it hit in the right spot. Then his pals joined in.

"He's trying to kill us. He's robbing us."

"Shoot the motherfucker before he shoots you, too." They started to get up, but the police made them stay put while they were cuffed.

Oscar was allowed to lower his arms to put on the handcuffs. Then they frisked him. He tried the lawyer thing. It had gotten him out of a few traffic tickets before.

"I'm an attorney, officer," he said to the young female cop who was leading him to the patrol car. "I was only protecting the lady and myself from being mugged, possibly killed."

She looked around, "What lady is that?" then opened the rear door of the car and pushed him in by the head.

"I have identification in my wallet," he said feebly, after the door closed.

In the back of the car, he realized how difficult it was to sit comfortably with his hands cuffed behind him. He had never been inside a police car before. He noticed there were no inside door handles on the back doors and there were actually bars on the windows and a plastic shield like in a taxi between the front and back seats. The inside of the car smelled like disinfectant.

Oscar noticed that the motor home was pulling out of the lot. It had an Indiana license plate. They would have quite a story to tell their neighbors when they got back home from vacation. He hoped it was the couple who had complained about the smoking.

Oscar was being interviewed in the cop car when Lucy came out. An ambulance had just pulled up for the wounded man. Three more police cars arrived and lights flashed all over the lot illuminating everything in red and blue. Cops were milling about. The unwounded bad guys had been put in other patrol cars. They opened the door to let Lucy speak to him.

"What are you doing in there?" she asked.

"They seem to think I did something wrong. I told them what happened, and I think they're sympathetic but say they have to take me in until they get it sorted out. Stick around and give them your statement."

"I'll follow you down there. I just wish you had shot the bastard in the balls."

"That's where I was aiming."

Rico sat in a van parked along the street next to the Ebb Tide parking lot watching to see how the whole scene played out. He was angry, but showed no outward sign. He took great pride in controlling his emotions. Mind and body, he often said, have to keep them pure. From the outside the tinted windows allowed no inside view of him. He had made a mistake hiring the punks. Should have taken care of it himself. They actually let that pussy lawyer take control of the situation, he thought, disgusted with them and himself. He had considered intervening, but the gunshot had changed the complexion of the situation.

No matter. There would be another opportunity to inter- rogate the woman. Rico drank his thermos of tea while waiting until the last cop car was gone, then started his van and rolled away.

Chapter Eight

After a night in jail, most of which Oscar spent in the detective's interview room explaining over and over to anyone who would listen his version of what had happened, they came to release him. As Oscar emptied the manila envelope on the counter to return the contents of his pockets to their former locations, he noticed the derringer was missing.

"What about my gun?" he asked the officer standing opposite him.

"Don't press your luck. We have to hold that as evidence for the prosecutor."

"You mean in the case against the guys who attacked me, right?"

"Maybe that. Maybe also in the assault charge to be filed against you. Or maybe in the CCW case against you. I'm letting you go, but expect to hear from the prosecutor after they decide what charges are going to be filed."

"I bought that gun legally."

"But you don't have a carry permit. It's easy enough to get a CCW, and you should have done it. Even my grandfather has one and he's in a wheelchair. Anyway, there should be a receipt for the gun in the paperwork I gave you. This is serious business. I suggest you get a lawyer. We have a referral number for you if you like." The young officer seemed to be suppressing a smirk. He was really getting off on putting it to a lawyer.

"I know how to hire an attorney, thank you. But I think you should understand that I'd rather face the penalty of carrying a concealed weapon than the alternative of having the woman abducted and raped and possibly both of us being killed. Plus we have the stand-your-ground law here, and as you know I had the right to shoot the guy if I felt threatened." Oscar tried to sound indignant, stuffed the rest of his things in his pants pockets, and turned to leave.

"You should get the CCW. I know what you're saying, but I have to do my job," the cop said to Oscar's retreating back. "We can't have frontier justice out there. But you might like to know that the guys who were after you have other warrants outstanding, so they'll likely be here for a while."

Oscar left the building after finding a rare pay telephone to call a taxi and waiting for it to take him to his car at the Ebb Tide. He had to duck out the back door to meet the cab to avoid the reporters he'd seen waiting for him in front. He regretted now not getting the concealed weapons permit. Florida had very lenient gun laws, and he could've had one just by filling out the form, taking a short class, and paying the fee.

Oscar wondered how Roy was doing. He hadn't seen Roy while he was in custody, but then he hadn't had the run of the place. Sydney would feed Jesse, but she said the dog acted despondent when left alone overnight. He remembered that was the way he used to feel when Sydney would take off on one of her unexplained trips, back before the breakup.

This was the first time Oscar had ever shot anyone, or had even shot *at* anyone. He kept the pistols in the cars because of the rapidly disintegrating state of law and order in southeast Florida. The high unemployment rate and rampant drug addiction were making a lot of people desperate and angry. He hadn't been sure he would actually have been able to use a gun on someone, but felt more comfortable with it than a whistle or a can of mace. He wasn't sorry for what he had done.

In fact, the experience gave him a rush. Made him feel like he was on amphetamines for the twelve hours or so after it happened. It felt good, and he also felt a little guilt just because it did feel good.

Is it easier the second time?

At the Ebb Tide he had the cab wait while he made sure the car started. He noticed as he was pulling out that the blood from the guy's knee was still pooled on the pavement, a dark smeary stain that looked like someone had spilled a pot of coffee.

Once home, he took a shower, fed and petted Jesse, whose whole body seemed to wag with the tail, walked him briefly in the back lot, tried unsuccessfully to find Sydney downstairs, then called her from the office.

"Sydney. It's Oscar."

"Did you get Roy out?"

"No. I'm working on it. Listen I have a mission for you. I need you to go down to the marina and check out Big Jack's death. See if you can find witnesses or people who knew Jack, whatever, then get back to me ASAP."

"Cool. I can be an investigator. Should I take a gun?"

"No. I have enough defendants right now. I have to change and get Judge Olivares to set up an arraignment. I'll talk to you later. Oh, and call that garage that worked on the Toyota last time. It needs another operation."

"Drive the Mustang, Oscar. It's the only decent car you own."

"I'm saving it. It's vintage. I can't use it for everyday, the miles add up too fast. How many times have we had this conversation?"

Oscar had bought the Mustang ten years earlier from a woman who had kept it nearly undriven in her garage since it was new. Technically it was a 1964 and a half. A white convertible with a black top, and he got it with only fifteen hundred miles on the odometer. He rarely drove it and it now registered just over thirty-two hundred. Every mile counted. He kept it covered under the carport in back of the building. The other cars he parked in the rutted sand of the garden.

He wandered into his studio and unwrapped the sculpture of Sydney. It was beginning to dry so he sprayed it with a mist of water, wrapped it in damp rags and recovered it with the plastic bag. He could keep it workable for several weeks this way if he paid attention to it. Now that he had to take care of his own legal problems as well as Roy's he expected it would be a while before he got back to doing any artwork. Jesse followed him from room to room, though he was now too old and arthritic to get up the stairs to the apartment.

Judge Olivares had agreed to do the arraignment at five at the jail, where there was a small courtroom for that purpose. He didn't promise bond and made Oscar do the work of scaring up a State's Attorney and court reporter. He made the calls, twisted some arms, and still had time for a nap before he had to go back to jail. It seemed he was spending more time there than at home. Unfortunately Sheila Katz was the on-call prosecutor.

Assistant state's attorney Sheila Katz would be angry that Oscar had brought her in to work on a Saturday. When Roy and Oscar were partners, Sheila had been a new assistant prosecutor and Oscar had had several misdemeanor trials opposite her. She hadn't ballooned up at that time, and Oscar had even dated her twice after his divorce. Things went sour when, as she termed it, he dumped her.

But as far as Oscar was concerned, they had been in a casual relationship with no commitments and no obligations, and she was the one, after all, who had pushed the concept of a no-strings, purely physical affair. Hey, he was a guy. Of course there were lots of strings thrown at him as time went on. He later thought of her as the transitional woman, the one who helped him appreciate living alone and allowing him to go to restaurants comfortably as a single.

Inevitably, she had changed her initially relaxed attitude after a short time, looking for more from him than he was willing to give. The end came when she arrived one afternoon with a cardboard box of her books to keep at his place. It felt to him like she was slowly moving in, and he put them back into her car when she left. A messy end, reinforcing his belief that not only was there no free lunch, there was also no free sex. So from then on whenever they met in court it was like facing a pit bull with a toothache. Pulling her away from her cats and television on a day off wasn't going to improve their relationship.

Oscar hoped that she wouldn't let their personal problems of the past interfere with her professional duties of the present. Roy shouldn't have to suffer jail over Oscar's relationship errors.

Chapter Nine

"I want to plead guilty, Oscar," Roy said.

"What? Say again slowly. But before you do, remember what we always told our clients at the defender's office: Never plead guilty unless you got a deal. Can you say that out loud?"

Oscar and Roy were back in the small conference room. No smoking allowed but the air smelled suspiciously of smoke. Roy had asked to talk to him privately before the arraignment started. The Judge, Sheila, the court reporter, and various deputies waited, presumably impatiently, in the larger room upstairs that served as a part-time courtroom for the jailhouse arraignments.

"I don't want to discuss it. If you can't do this for me I'll ask that you be dismissed and I'll represent myself."

"Roy, Roy, Roy." Oscar shook his head and fell back into one of the chairs. "This is a capital offense. You know what that means. We have the death penalty in this state. They haven't asked for it, but might. Use your head. Even if you want to plead I can likely get you second-degree with no trouble. You wouldn't even serve the full term. And why plead to anything? Did you kill Jack?"

"That's what I'm going to say. I have my reasons."

"Tell me about them." Oscar's voice was harsh, and he was getting angry.

"I told you I can't discuss it. Believe me when I tell you that you and Lucy and everybody else will be a lot better off if you leave it alone." He was pacing nervously, wiping his face with his palms and had somewhere found a damp, rumpled cigarette that he carried unlit.

"Have you talked to Lucy since you got in here?"

"Yes. I called her."

"And what did she tell you?"

"Nothing that concerns you. Just do what I ask."

"Okay," Oscar said, pushing away from the table. "But give me some time first. Stand mute at the bail hearing, and you can always plead later on. I have a few things to check out, and you should think about this very carefully. You have nothing to lose and everything to gain by giving it a little time."

Roy looked like he was going to cry. Much as Oscar tried to be a sensitive, liberated kind of guy, it irritated him to see a man in tears. Oscar thought that his attitude was the result of early exposure to John Wayne movies on late night TV. The Duke would never let anybody see him cry, that's for sure. And what was with this pleading guilty stuff? Roy knew better.

Oscar felt the tightening in his gut as they walked to the arraignment room. Despite having done hundreds of arraignments and more trials than he cared to count, any court appearance did this to him. He rehearsed what he would say, and began assembling his trial strategy. What defenses would he use? What motions would have to be made? Should Roy testify? The back of his neck began to tighten up, the precursor to a violent headache. He cursed softly at himself. This was just a fucking arraignment. Nothing at all, as court hearings went. What was wrong with him?

They went upstairs, and the judge set bail at two hundred thousand, against Oscar's protests. But Sheila had argued for no bail at all. The judge said that he thought the bail was low given the seriousness of the alleged offense, but that since Mr. Flagler was a member of the Bar and a respected member of the community, he was giving him a break. Roy said he could arrange it, and at that Oscar snapped his briefcase shut and turned to leave. He had learned that once a judge gives you what you want, leave the room quickly before he changes his mind. Roy was taken out by the elbows by two deputies to be returned to his cell pending the posting of the bond. No one else moved.

"Mr. Leopold? One moment if you will. While you're here the state's attorney suggested we clear up one other little matter."

"Your Honor?" Oscar said, turning back to the judge and looking over at Sheila who smiled at him. A bad sign.

The bailiff read from a court file, "People of the State of Florida versus Oscar Leopold, case number 713543."

Sheila stood.

"Your honor, Sheila Katz for the people. We are here for the arraignment of Mr. Oscar Leopold on the felony charges of assault with a deadly weapon, carrying a concealed weapon, and unlawful discharge of a firearm." She stepped over and handed Oscar a sheaf of papers.

"How do you wish to plead on these charges, Mr. Leopold?" asked the judge. "You have the right to an attorney, as I am sure you know, and the state will appoint an attorney for you if you're unable to afford one."

Judge Olivares seemed embarrassed. Sheila had a smirking half smile on her face.

"Is this some kind of joke?" Oscar asked, thinking that she was pushing this personal grudge a little too far.

"This is very serious, as are all felony cases," replied the judge. "I have read the report and the complaint by the alleged victims while you were downstairs. Now how do you wish to plead? Let's get this over with."

Oscar felt his face go hot as he realized they were indeed serious. He had never been a defendant before and despite his familiarity with the system had to admit he was a bit scared, yet angry at the same time. He restrained himself, knowing that while he had a high tolerance level, once pushed too far he could become irrationally angry, even violent.

"I object to this whole proceeding as being irregular. I haven't even been booked, and this is the first I've heard of these charges.

The procedure is defective, and I want this thing dismissed right now," Oscar said quickly and perhaps too loudly.

"If you prefer, Mr. Leopold, I can have the bailiff take you down to booking, go through the whole process, then bring you back here. Of course that will mean I'll miss my tee time and will be setting bail later this afternoon instead of now. What would you like to do?"

"I withdraw my objection, your honor," said Oscar, defeated.

Oscar's bail was set at twenty-five thousand dollars with 10 percent cash or surety. He called Sydney and she arranged to get him out. Roy's bail required a trip to the bank on Monday. Roy didn't want to pay the bondsman's fee to get out early.

Sheila was still in the building and stopped to see Oscar while he waited for the bail arrangements. He was in the small holding cell near the front desk.

"Oscar," she said sweetly, "I think this environment suits you." She was standing looking in at him. He had been sitting on the concrete bench with his head in his hands.

"Go fuck yourself, Sheila. No one else will." He didn't look up.

"I just wanted to tell you that the judge wouldn't like it if you're caught with any firearms in your possession while this case is pending."

"No shit." Oscar stood and approached her. She backed away a step even though the bars separated them.

"Tell me, Sheila, did you request this case or was it just assigned to you?"

"Luck of the draw, Leopold. Luck of the draw." She grinned, turned triumphantly, and left. That night she would celebrate Oscar's incarceration by treating her three cats to canned tuna.

Chapter Ten

Meeting Oscar for the first time had been pure chance. Sydney fled Philadelphia after a job went bad, with the police and the client searching for her. She needed a place to live and, preferably, some cover. The situation in Philly had been ideal. She was the resident manager at a small motel, so didn't need to get housing or utilities in her name. Housekeeping was done by a local mother and daughter who would fill in if she had to go on a mission. She was off the grid. But unforeseen things can happen no matter how careful the plan—like a son making a surprise visit to his father, who at the time was being drowned in his pool by Sydney. She escaped, and wasn't sure anyone knew her name, but they had her description, and that was enough to cause her to leave town, not even going back to the motel to pick up her belongings.

She needed a similar setup in Florida, so when she stumbled across the help wanted sign in the window of the Rose Madder Gallery, she went in. Oscar was easy to charm, she got the job, and the room downstairs came with it. He didn't ask for references or a resumé. A likeable, laid-back kind of guy who took her at her word. So it worked out well. The relationship expanded to moving upstairs with him. She had always had a hard time having a friendship with a guy if it didn't involve romance and sex, and he didn't seem to mind. But after three months of living like a couple, sharing the bathroom, bumping into each other in the morning, she moved back to her room. They hadn't argued or fought. It was more like a moving out on your roommate. No hard feelings, she just wasn't ready. So she did her best to maintain the friendship for personal and business purposes, and it was working so far. They were indeed friends, and there was no sexual tension on her part even when she posed for him.

Sunday afternoon Sydney was to work in the gallery with Oscar. He was uncrating the wooden boxes containing the paintings from a Chicago artist for the show that was opening in the gallery in two weeks. The rechargeable electric screw gun had enough juice for the first fifty screws, then died. He was plugging it back into the charger when Sydney came in through the office, having come in the side door from the alley.

"Sydney, I told you to come in through the studio. You track up my carpet. Besides, I might have confidential papers lying around."

"I wipe my feet. You have no secrets from me, anyway." She put her motorcycle helmet away and came back to the gallery.

The building had housed a variety of businesses before he took it over, including an auto parts store, pizzeria, antique shop, a T-shirt screen printing company, and, just before he bought it, a co-op gallery for local artists. It was concrete block and stucco, what the real estate people called CBS, and had been painted various shades of pastel over the years. Most of them showed through the layers of peel.

A New Orleans style wrought-iron balcony hung over the sidewalk in front opening to the apartment upstairs. He installed a law office on the ground floor using part of the gallery space. The alley next to the building led to a private overgrown enclosed garden in the rear where he parked his cars. Nearby, a rusting, vine-covered pile was what had once been a garden shed and tools. He stayed away from it after seeing a large rattlesnake slither inside one day.

The gallery took up the front third of the building. It had high ceilings with track lighting and a polished oak floor. Large glass display windows and a glass door faced the sidewalk. Two doors were in the rear wall. One led to Oscar's law office, a single room with carpeting, a desk, file cabinet, computer, and three chairs, and the other to his studio. Behind the studio was a workroom with an electric ceramics kiln, toilet, back door, and Sydney's space. The stairway to upstairs was in the studio. He had changed the name of the gallery to the Rose Madder Gallery. This caused some confusion among non-art people who didn't know rose madder was a color, not a person's name. They often asked to see Ms. Madder.

"You mean you finally got a client—besides Roy?" she asked. Her voice was throaty and raspy, like that of a heavy smoker—Janis Joplin-like, though Oscar had never seen her light one up. She was drinking Pepsi from a two-liter plastic bottle and jumped up to sit on the nearest crate. She was wearing scuffed snakeskin cowboy boots and jeans despite the heat. A gold ring in one nostril was connected by a thin chain to a matching ring in her right ear. Her small unbra'd breasts were clearly visible through the thin material of the white tank top, just a hint of nipple.

"Two. Me and Roy." He accepted a slug of Sydney's Pepsi.

"Yeah. I heard about your Clint Eastwood trick over at the Ebb Tide."

"I don't remember Dirty Harry getting busted when he shot the bad guys."

"You want me to see that the complaining witnesses don't show up for court?" Sydney didn't smile when she said it and Oscar thought she was kidding.

"Forget it. I can take care of it. I think this is just a case of Sheila Katz being pissed at me. A payback for the misery she thinks I've caused her. I'll probably have to grovel convincingly and kiss her ass and she'll give it up. So did you find out anything down at the Marina?"

"Sure did." Sydney drank the rest of the Pepsi and continued, "That was one hell of an explosion. Wrecked two other boats and took out a big chunk of the dock. They hauled what was left of Big Jack's boat out and into the yard. It burned before it sank.

There wasn't much to see there. I found a witness who didn't see the actual explosion but heard it. He said he saw them pull big Jack's body out of the wreckage. Said he looked like a wet burned marshmallow and didn't know how they identified him. The poor kid who was killed in the explosion floated downriver and was found by the Marine Patrol near the inlet."

Oscar had found a regular Phillips head screwdriver and was now trying to extract the screws from the wooden case.

"Did you talk to any of the cops?"

"Yeah. One of the Marine Patrol officers. Not the detectives. I think they hide out on weekends. I tried the Coast Guard, but they wouldn't talk to me. The Marine Patrol guy said they had to identify Jack's body forensically. The clothes, jewelry, and so forth were Jack's and the forensics matched up."

"You mean he was so bad that they had to use dental records or DNA?"

"No, dental was unavailable, but they did use DNA on the body using hair samples from the house for comparison and Jack's wife identified the body before the cremation. That must have been tough. It took some time to get clearance from the state for the cremation, but that's done now. It also turns out he had a wound to the head inflicted before the fire. He was already dead when it blew up."

The screwdriver slipped out of its slot and Oscar's hand cracked into the shipping case, skinning his knuckles.

"Damn! This is why I don't do manual labor. I always end up cut and bleeding." He sucked on his wound while Sydney picked up the screwdriver from the floor.

"You're so fucking inept. Let me do this for you." Sydney finished turning the screw out, having no trouble doing so. Oscar was chagrined. He was the guy and using tools was supposed to be in his area of expertise. She weighed all of a hundred pounds and the top of her head only came to his shoulder.

"I am, too, ept. Mechanical things just are not my deal. My eptness lies elsewhere," Oscar said. Sydney looked up and smiled, handing him back the screwdriver.

"Then there was the diesel fuel thing. I found out that not only had someone cut the fuel line, but that it was no accident that gasoline was mixed with the diesel. Everybody else in the marina got good fuel. Jack's boat was the only one with the gas in it."

"Do you have any good news?"

"Well, yes. They couldn't place you at the scene of the crime." She grinned.

"Maybe in Jersey that's funny. Me, I'm not laughing."

Sydney's story of her background as told to Oscar was of necessity different from fact. She told him that she was from Newark and had been in the periphery of the neighborhood street gangs there. She had been living with a friend, an art dealer in Manhattan on the Lower East side, when the woman died unexpectedly. The woman's relatives evicted her, allowing her to take just her clothes. A friend in Florida saw an advertisement for an art gallery manager and called her. Sydney came and got the job. Oscar swallowed the story whole. She thought the cuteness factor worked in her favor. Guys.

Oscar went out the back door. Two butts were sticking out of the open hood of his Toyota. It looked like his friendly part-time mechanic had a helper.

Angelo Gonzalez lived down the alley in a concrete block single-level flat-roofed house with a sandy yard full of kids and two scraggly banana trees.

Oscar looked in with them at the grease-covered engine.

"Any hope, do you think?"

Angelo straightened up and wiped his hands on the embroidered setting sun on the front of his coveralls. The helper was working with a wrench down in the depths and glanced at them with a greasy gap-toothed grin as he worked.

"Looks like the timing chain." Angelo waited for Oscar to say something.

Oscar thought, what the hell is a timing chain? But he had learned the appropriate response.

"How much and how long will it take?"

"Five hundred and two days." Angelo wiped his hands again on the front of his coveralls, grinned, and crossed his arms. Wiping them on the coveralls was futile since they had more grease on them than the hands.

"Christ! That's more than the car's worth!"

"What's it worth if you don't fix it?" It was a familiar conversation.

He left them alone and went looking for Sydney. She was in her room. Oscar could hear some old seventies psychedelic rock coming from behind the steel door. He knocked loudly. The music shut off. The door opened and Sydney squeezed out, locking it behind her. What was in there?

"Will you talk to Angelo for me? See if I'm being screwed over the repairs? The whole car isn't worth more than the fix. He says it's some kind of timer chain."

"Timing chain."

"Whatever."

Oscar hated new cars or anything else that required a regular monthly payment. Too much pressure to make the money. Keeping the overhead low kept the life simple, so nowadays he always had at least two used cars, figuring that one of them should work most of the time.

He went back to his office and tried to find the legal form for a discovery motion on the computer. He thought he might be able to adapt one he had used before. There were good programs available with every conceivable form on them, but in his quest to keep the expenses down he didn't have one of those. The best he could do was try to save what he had done previously and recycle it if another client came by with a similar problem. The truth was he had lost interest in practicing law and did the necessary minimum to keep expenses paid when the art income didn't cover them. So keeping up to date in office technology wasn't high on the priority list.

He heard the buzzer go off, indicating someone was coming in the front door of the gallery. Jesse starting barking, telling Oscar he wasted the money on the buzzer.

Damn. He thought he had locked it. It was likely either another newsperson or a gallery customer. Legal clients ordinarily called first, and his friends knew to come to the back door. Sydney kidded him about having a storefront business that was never open. It could be he was just not cut out for either law or the retail business.

Customers annoyed him.

A tall man in his fifties, with an island-shaped shiny bald spot and wearing a tan suit stood looking at the two paintings that Oscar had managed to extricate from their packing cases and propped against the wall. Jesse had managed to get up and smelled the man's trouser legs and crotch. He turned and tried to push Jesse away. Not a dog owner.

"We're not really open." Oscar stepped into the room.

"Mr. Leopold?" The man turned and extended his hand. Oscar hoped it wasn't a potential client. He rarely got walk-in legal business and didn't encourage it. Most of them wanted divorce or child support work done, high-stress stuff better left to the younger lawyers.

"Yes. Can I help you Mr.,…"

"My name is Ames. Clifford Ames. I'm working for Atlantic Coast and Gulf Insurance?"

Oscar wasn't sure what his question was so he answered him anyway.

"I suppose you do."

Ames looked confused. Oscar shook his hand.

"We're primarily a life insurance company. We had a policy on Jack Gamble?"

"Ah," Oscar replied eloquently. Ames smiled, thinking apparently that he now had Oscar's attention.

"I'm investigating the circumstances of Mr. Gamble's death. It's pretty standard procedure in a case of this size."

"What size is that?"

"Actually we have two policies totaling two point five million dollars."

"Ah."

"Yes. So in any event we have to check out the circumstances to be sure we have liability."

"The guy's dead. Why wouldn't you have had liability?"

"Suicide, for instance. The policies are less than a year old. If it was suicide we wouldn't have to pay."

"How about homicide?"

"Of course, that's what the police say and I'm inclined to go along with them. If, for instance, the beneficiary were involved, then of course the proceeds would be payable to another next of kin or heir. A murderer can't legally collect life insurance proceeds on the victim."

"I know. So why are you telling me this."

"I understand you're representing the alleged killer, who is not the beneficiary by the way, but I thought you might have some information about the defendant's relationship with Lucy Gamble, the wife and the beneficiary."

"Word travels fast. I only entered my appearance yesterday."

He smiled inscrutably. "We have our sources."

"I am sure you do. Like the radio and television, for instance. Thanks for coming by." Oscar started toward the door, expecting Ames to follow so he could let him out and make sure the door was locked this time. Ames didn't follow so Oscar had to turn back toward him, but had his hand on the door handle.

"Were they close?"

"Close? They were married."

"I mean intimate, in love? Some couples aren't you know."

"I don't know. Or care. They worked together. I really know nothing about Big Jack except what I got from the police. And anything I know about my client is confidential."

"Nothing?"

"Nothing." He opened the door. This time Ames stepped toward it and stopped just before going through the doorway.

"I'm defending my friend and former partner for the guy's murder. Gamble was no friend of mine. I didn't even like his commercials, and I hated his style of law. So I guess I can't help you. Thanks for stopping by."

Ames exited, but Oscar reopened the door to take the proffered business card Ames was pointing at him, then reclosed the
door and made sure it was locked this time.

Two and a half million bucks. Ah. Things were beginning
to get interesting.

Oscar hadn't yet checked out Jack's client, Cake, the one that
had been harassing the office, and decided not to put it off any
longer. He found the notes with the guy's name and address
that he had gotten from the office with Lucy's help and called
his number. No answer. The address was over on Skees Road.
Near enough for a cold call.

Chapter Eleven

Sydney sat alone behind her locked door reviewing Rico's email with the information on the new target. The hit he had substituted was for another lawyer. He gave the details as to work patterns, family relationships, home, club, and office addresses, drinking and social habits, hobbies—even an attached photo. He gave a detailed explanation of the crooked deals the lawyer had been involved in, the clients he had ripped off plus the names of his last two mistresses and an allegation he beat his wife. All to make it look like a justifiable hit, she supposed. None of it might be true. Investigation was in order. Of Rico. Rico said his father was a lawyer and he had some sort of connection with these other two. The photo of the target was attached to the email as a jpeg. It showed the guy at a party, probably a bar association function, based on the way others in the background were dressed. He looked drunk. Rico was demanding to know the date she was going to carry out the new contract.

It took an hour of searching but she located him. She first checked details of the sender's email, and got his IP address using an IP locater tool available online. Google had one which actually gave a printable map. This led, through another program she had, to his computer's location and through other search programs to him, Richard (Rico) Walters. His father Robert Jerome Walters was senior partner of Walters, Schaefer, and Gregg in Fort Lauderdale. There was little information on

Rico except for a couple of arrests for assault, no convictions. Daddy's connections no doubt helped with that. The law firm did mostly corporate and insurance litigation. Not like Big Jack's sleazy operation. She found Rico's property ownership records. He had two places in South Florida. The tax collector's office showed ownership of several cars, a boat, and a van. Married but no children. He was thirty-two years old, white, and she knew he was an asshole. There was even a picture of him on the law firm's website, posing with the staff. A big guy with a smirk.

A similar check on her would give him nothing. The only link would be the number of the dead cell phone and he must have bribed or beaten the guy at the mail drop to give it up.

She had to go check it out.

She made good time on her Harley Sportster. Even though wearing a helmet was optional in Florida, she always wore one after a minivan had turned into her three years ago. The helmet had cracked open instead of her skull. She was a believer now.

She parked across from the store, watched the place for a time, checking out parked cars and anyone loitering. Anyone who might be watching for her. Looked like it was all clear, no pedestrians, no one in the parked cars, and just medium traffic on the main street. She thought once again of getting another outfit for riding the bike. Wearing all black in the intense sun was a heat sponge. She carried the helmet and walked across the street for a final mail check. She would be changing the mail drop now that it might be compromised.

There were two customers in the shop, one having a package weighed and another using the copy machine. Paul, the owner, was there but seemed in fine health, so it must have been a bribe rather than a beating that got Rico her email and cell number. Couldn't have been any other way.

Two envelopes this time. One of them was red and large. Both were bulky enough to contain cash. She stuck them inside her jacket and made a roundabout way home. She remembered a line from a movie that went something like, "Don't fall into patterns. Your enemies might ambush you." Actually, good advice in her line of work. On the way back to the gallery she stopped at a Wendy's for a salad lunch. It wasn't fine cuisine, but quick and low fat. Two men, both wearing untucked Cuban shirts and sunglasses followed her in, but hadn't ordered any food. One took a seat in the corner facing her, the other went back outside. Uh-oh. Could be trouble.

She gulped down her salad and walked out quickly, starting her bike and making many quick turns back toward home, hoping to lose any tail. She was sure she hadn't been followed from the mail drop so there was only one way those guys found her. Halfway home she pulled behind a gas station, got off the bike, and inspected it carefully. A small square electronic look-ing box was magnetically adhered to the bottom of the engine. Probably a GPS. Two things she could do. Leave it there and set a trap for them, or ditch it.

She pulled it off, drove over to the gas pumps, and casually stuck it to the underside of the car ahead of her whose driver had gone inside the station.

Someone was trying to track her down. Probably Rico. It was time for a change of plans.

Chapter Twelve

The address was in a run-down trailer park, not an apartment complex as Oscar had envisioned. Twenty narrow aluminum-sided trailers hauled down from the North in the fifties and sixties stood in two long rows on either side of the road going in. They were the ten and twelve foot wide models that were too worn and shabby to go into the newer retirement parks where they called them manufactured housing instead of trailers. The narrow road, paved with crumbling asphalt, crushed shell, and sand, was lined with broken-down cars, shedding Australian pines, and plastic garbage cans. Children played in the street, stopping to watch him as he drove through trying to find the address. Not all the lots were marked with numbers but one of the children pointed out Cake's place for him.

Oscar drove around a big yellow cat sleeping in the middle of the road, parked under a drooping cabbage palm, and took off his jacket. The temperature was already up to the high eighties, and there was no air conditioning in the car. His shirt was soaked with sweat, and it felt good to get out into a little breeze. Cake's trailer had the words Parkwood Executive in worn chrome lettering above the front windows near the flat roofline. It no longer gave the executive image intended at manufacture.

The green and white aluminum siding was faded and streaked with dirt. Two of the crank-open, jalousie type window panels in front were replaced with cardboard. The underside was shielded intermittently with plywood sheeting, the peeling paint of which looked like it had once been a close match to the green of the trailer. Broken bottles, tattered plastic garbage bags, and old lawn chairs were stored underneath around the stacked concrete blocks supporting the trailer. In the back of the littered narrow yard was a rusting steel storage shed with an ominous dark interior and no door.

Oscar walked up the sidewalk, stepped over a collapsed Weber barbecue kettle and rapped on the screen door. He stood back where Cake could see him. He couldn't see the face clearly through the rusting screen when it appeared.

"Yeah? What do you want?"

"My name is Oscar Leopold. I'm an attorney. Are you Mr. Carl Cake?"

He opened the door and squinted at Oscar.

"Kind of bright out here. Yeah, I'm Cake. If you work for my ex-wife you can tell her I got no more money to give her. She took all I had, and there ain't no more."

He stood holding the screen door open. Oscar had expected a slovenly sort of appearance given the neighborhood and the condition of the housing, but Cake, though unshaven, was neatly dressed. He was thin, in his mid fifties, with a full head of white hair and wearing gray slacks and a yellow short-sleeved shirt. He looked like an emaciated and seedy Arnold Palmer.

"I don't work for your wife. I'm defending the man accused of murdering your lawyer, Jack Gamble. Would you mind answering a few questions?"

Carl stepped out onto the small concrete porch, thought for a second, then extended his hand to Oscar as he came down the steps. Oscar shook the hand, realizing as he grasped it that something was wrong. He was holding only part of a hand. The thumb and forefinger were missing. He resisted the impulse to pull away, and looked Carl right in the eye.

Oscar made a point of not looking at the hand and Cake held for maybe a moment too long. The experience reminded Oscar of shaking hands left-handed with a man whose right arm was missing or disabled. Not quite right, but you tried to pretend it was perfectly natural so as not to embarrass the other guy or yourself.

Oscar fished a business card out of his wallet and handed it to over. Cake sat on the steps examining the card, then found his cigarettes in his shirt pocket. He lit one with a stick match scratched on the side of the wrought iron porch rail and threw the flaming match onto the ground.

"I already talked to the cops. I didn't have nothing to do with the killing, but I'm glad the bastard's dead. Saved me the trouble of doing it myself." He handed the card back, then absentmindedly flicked the ashes from his cigarette into the cuff of his pants. A portable ashtray. Oscar noticed that he was wearing expensive looking shoes.

"You were a client of his, I understand?"

"One of my bigger mistakes. I saw his ad on the TV and called about my accident." He held out his right hand again, holding it up in what would have been the old sixties peace sign, but with the missing fingers it looked to Oscar more like a bird's foot than it did a human hand.

"Cut 'em off in the lawnmower. Damn thing didn't shut off automatically like it was supposed to. He was suing for me. We was supposed to get a couple hundred thousand. That's what I agreed to, but he kept stalling me when it was time to get the money. Then he says the case was over, and I lost. But I never even went to court! Son of a bitch wouldn't even talk to me after that." He spat into the sand near Oscar's feet.

"No offense to you, mister, but I think you lawyers are all a bunch of scum-sucking pigs." He smiled. His teeth were yellow tobacco-stained.

"I've heard that opinion before. Did you ever visit him at home?" Oscar would have preferred to do this business in the shade, but had no desire to go inside the trailer.

"Would of, if I knew where he lived. You can ask. I did for sure visit the office. Probably lives in some fancy place he bought with my money. But I was going to get even all right. I filed papers against him with the lawyers club so he'd get kicked out. I got another lawyer suing to get my money back, too. The damned cops wouldn't do anything for me."

"Do the police suspect that you had anything to do with his death?" Oscar felt for his car keys just in case he needed a quick getaway now that the hard questions were being asked.

"I don't give a rat's ass if they do. I was at the hospital with an infection, so I got an alibi. I wouldn't of killed him anyway. How could I get my money back if he's dead? Say, you being a lawyer, maybe you can answer that one for me."

"I'd call my lawyer if I were you. It may be that there's some money coming from the Florida Bar Association or maybe he had some kind of malpractice insurance. Wouldn't hurt to check."

Cake stood and stretched.

"You better go now, Mr. Lawyer. Can't say it was nice talking to you. If your guy did kill him, tell him thanks from me."

"I appreciate your time, Mr. Cake." Oscar went back to the car, shooing the kids off the hood where they had been sitting watching the conversation. Oscar thought they looked a bit disappointed since there had been no fight. He checked to be sure he had all his hubcaps before he drove off, then remembered that he had never had hubcaps.

Chapter Thirteen

By late Monday afternoon Sydney had arranged Roy's bail, and then dropped him off at his house on her way back to the gallery. Oscar was polishing the Mustang when she pulled around the back of the building. It was eighty-eight degrees and humid. Oscar wore his Detroit Tigers ball cap, shorts, an unbuttoned red and green parrot-covered Hawaiian shirt and tennis shoes with no socks. He rarely wore socks except in extremely formal circumstances.

"You should drive that thing once in a while. Keep it in shape."

In her white shorts and open-necked red blouse she looked more appealing, he thought, than she did nude. He used 'naked' when he was talking about sex and "nude" when in the art mode. He really believed he could make the distinction, regardless of what Sydney said.

When Sydney modeled she teasingly accused him of being turned on. She said it wouldn't do him any good, but she could understand how he would find it difficult to resist her. Truth was that Sydney was short and thin with a hard boyish figure. Not Oscar's type he tried to tell himself, though he had had no complaints when they were a couple.

Oscar picked the car cover up off the ground, shook off the leaves and sand, and held one end out to her.

"Help me cover it up."

"Sure you don't want to take me for a spin first?" She leaned over the car teasingly, apparently knowing her tiny cleavage would show off well that way. "I could take you for a ride. You could let me drive this time."

"Not today," Oscar said, proud of his restraint and professionalism.

"I have a way of helping you with Roy's case. Want to hear more?"

"Any help is good help at this point. Right now help me with this, and then we can go inside and talk where it's cool."

They snapped the cover over the Mustang and went back inside. Oscar noticed that his Toyota was no longer in the yard, and the Buick was again covered with tangerines, dead branches, and leaves. He made another mental note to have Angelo cut the tree down.

He fed Jesse, putting the bowl in front of him so he wouldn't have to get up. At seventeen, the dog was elderly and Oscar hoped he would last even longer. The problem was that he was nearly blind, partly deaf, and suffered from occasional incontinence. He went upstairs to his apartment. Sydney had offered to, as she put it, "solve the Jesse problem" for him, but he declined.

"Want some coffee?" he asked. Sydney had followed and was trying to find a piece of furniture not covered with clothes, books, or dirty dishes. She finally picked up a pile from an armchair, and tossed it onto the couch to clear a space to sit. She waited while Oscar made the coffee in his new plunger pot. He'd experimented with every coffee maker type he could find to get the best coffee in the shortest possible time. In the morning every second counted. Next to instant, this method was his current choice. He'd even bought an automatic pot, and hooked it up to a timer, but never remembered to set it up the night before.

"None for me."

"So what can you do to help?" He watched the water try to boil.

"I found a way to get into Jack's office and look around. Ask some questions. I don't know specifically what I would be looking for, but anything that might help Roy. His relationship with Jack. And with Lucy. What enemies and business relationships he might have. I could come up with a complete personal profile on the guy."

"Sounds good enough, real private-eye-like, but how do you propose to do that? It's a private office, not a public library." The water was finally bubbling, so he pulled it off the burner and poured it into the jar over the coffee grounds, counted to fifteen, and forced the plunger to the bottom.

"That should be easy. Lucy already asked me to help out at the office. She said things are in a big mess with the way Jack kept the records and the associates all fighting to claim as many files for themselves as they can. In the meantime there are court dates to keep, accountants to deal with, clients, and cops all over the place. And even though Roy's not working there anymore, I could suggest that I liaison with her on his cases to wrap them up or farm them out."

"I didn't know you and Lucy were friends." Oscar poured the coffee into two mismatched mugs, forgetting that she'd declined.

"Roy said they need temporary help at the office until things get sorted out. He called Lucy and arranged it. Personally I don't care for her, she's so full of herself. Uses too much perfume. Patchouli. I hate that. Roy likes her, though."

"Roy likes anything reasonably female."

"Look who's talking."

"I'm very selective. They have to be over eighteen, under eighty and weigh less than three hundred pounds—well, three-fifty."

"I think it would really be ironic and funny if you—the fat hater—ended up that way yourself when you get older. Anyway, she agreed to let me help out. I'm pretty good with computers so that's going to be my job."

"I think you have a plan. Keep me posted. I have to get over and see Roy, then stop in to the state's attorney to see about getting this bullshit criminal charge against me dismissed."

"I can text you—oops, forgot that you're technology chal-
lenged."

"Use the telephone and I promise I'll carry mine with me."

When Sydney checked her email she found two new messages
from Rico. No getting around it. Decision time.

Chapter Fourteen

Rancho Verde Estates was one of the hundreds of new subdivisions built inland from Lake Worth on ground that once had been part of the Everglades. The houses were roofed in red cement tile made to simulate terra cotta and came in only three styles of stuccoed concrete block. Each had four—not three or five, but four—newly transplanted cabbage palm trees in the small yards, sodded lawns, and a recreation center with shared pool. The pastel houses were huge but the lots were small. It was almost possible to stand between two houses and touch each with outstretched arms.

Oscar was reminded of a beehive when he drove through the streets, crowded with one after another nearly identical building. The occasional alligator and snake visited. A bigger problem was the oversized pythons and iguanas—former pets that became too much for their owners and were released to grow and breed. The pythons ate small dogs and cats and the iguanas devoured the landscape plants. Then there were the wild hogs that bulldozed lawns and golf courses. Man versus nature and nature wasn't going down easily.

Roy lived on a corner lot in the Elegante four bedroom model with attached screened "Florida Room" around the back. Oscar found him asleep in shorts and hairy bare belly in the Mexican woven rope hammock. The sliding door was unlocked. An opera, Verde, Oscar thought, played softly from the outdoor patio speakers. He went on into the kitchen, uncapped two cold Coronas, then found Roy had sitting in a patio chair with elbows on knees and forehead in hands.

"Here. This should chase away those evil jailhouse blues." He offered the beer. Roy took it and sat back.

"You should talk. Maybe we can share a cell."

"It's a bunch of crap. I'll never see the inside."

Roy laughed weakly, and Oscar told him the story of what he had decided to call *The Incident at Ebb Tide.*

"I told you carrying those guns in your cars would get you in trouble one day."

"I think it got me out of more trouble than I got into. And anybody who doesn't carry a gun around here nowadays is suicidal. So tell me about your insane plan to plead guilty.".

Roy looked at the floor and shook his head. "It's Lucy. I think she did it and I can't let her go to jail. I know it sounds crazy but I'll do this for her."

"What? Is this love? News to me, but it doesn't change anything. I 'm still your attorney of record and your friend. Do you think she'll let you take the fall for this? If she would then you are a fool. I predict after a couple of years on death row you'll regret this. And Lucy will be just a memory. We both know you didn't kill Big Jack. At least I'm pretty sure of it—it's hard to tell anything for sure these days. So tell me what you plan on telling the judge when he takes the plea you want to offer."

"I'll tell him I cut the fuel line and blew up the boat because he wouldn't make me partner."

"That's not enough. How did you do it?"

"I set the ignition so it would spark when he turned the key, igniting the fumes."

"You don't know shit about ignitions. And I found out he was dead before the explosion anyway."

Roy said nothing and got up for more beer.

"Okay. So you don't want to talk about it. You know that any kind of conviction, even on a lesser charge if we got the best plea deal in town with no jail means your license. No more law practice."

Roy shrugged.

"Tell me some other things then. What do you know about Big Jack's financial condition? For instance, did you know about the IRS? Was the firm in financial trouble?"

"I always thought we were doing real well. The expenses were high. I don't imagine television advertising comes cheap. And there was the staff. We had one paralegal and one word processor person for each attorney. But we turned over a lot of money. I personally settled several big cases last year that brought in over one point six million in fees."

"How were you paid?"

"Sort of like a salesman. Salary plus commission. I got a percentage of my gross intake scaled up as the dollars increased. I've done well but felt I deserved a bigger share like he promised when I went with him."

Roy and Oscar had discussed the idea of his taking the position with Big Jack before Roy accepted the offer. Jack didn't have a great reputation. He ran loud, garish ads on late night television reminiscent of appliance or car salespeople. He had toll-free twenty-four hour numbers, offered home and hospital visits, and even used an animated cartoon Spanish version of his pitch. The judges and other attorneys loathed him, but he seemed to make a lot of money and was able to pay top salaries in a time when many lawyers were looking for other work.

In the end it was the money that decided it. Roy was still married to his first wife and they both wanted the cash. Now she got it in the alimony that he had included in the judgment without her asking. His guilt offering to get the divorce through. Roy divorced his wife a year after Oscar's divorce was final.

"What about the IRS and financial trouble?"

"I knew about that, but it wasn't the kind of thing you could talk to him about. You know how he was. Real loudmouthed and superficial. But very private. I heard it was a big land deal in Texas, shopping centers and the like. Some small corporation he invested in. He was supposed to have taken big losses. I saw some of the paperwork and everybody was speculating about it in the office but we assumed he wouldn't get hurt. He knows, knew, that is, enough about the law to protect himself.

"The most serious problem he had was the bar association. There were at least three serious complaints against him alleging misuse of his client trust account. And there was an allegation that he had actually forged a client signature on a settlement check. We had talked about my becoming partner immediately to keep the firm together in case he was suspended. He denied any wrongdoing, of course, but said he wanted to keep everything covered. Then a few days before he died he said our deal was off. He said he was taking care of the problem.

"I blew up. I couldn't help it. When he hired me the arrangement was that he would make me partner in one year if my performance was satisfactory. Well, I made him a shitload of money, and the time was long up. He said he never intended to make me partner, the son of a bitch. He said that I must have misunderstood, but that if I was unhappy he would write me a nice letter of recommendation." Roy's face was red, and he was sweating again. He wiped his hand from forehead to chin.

"Did you threaten him?"

"I may have. I was hot, I know that. I should have punched him in the office when he slapped me—but I was so stunned I couldn't believe he had done it."

"What do you know about Jack and Lucy?"

"Just what everybody else does, I guess. He opened the office here six years ago, starting advertising big time immediately, and his practice took off. Until he had to hire associates to do the trial work that he couldn't bargain away, we all called him 'Make Me an Offer Jack' for his desire to settle a case at any cost to stay out of court. As far as I know he never went to trial on a case.

"The thing was, lately he seemed to have an uncanny ability to get maximum settlements for cases that seemed weak. I always expected the defense firms to call him on it and make him go to trial but they never did. The cases he handled himself always brought in the most money. It was almost as if the defense firms rolled over and played dead when he took a case."

"What about before six years ago?"

"I don't know. Lucy once or twice referred to having lived in Apalachicola."

"Up in the panhandle area?"

"Yes. Right on the Gulf. In fact, Lucy would sometimes start to talk about things that happened there and then would clam up, but I don't know if Jack was with her then. It was like she was hiding her past and Big Jack's. You could check with the bar association. They have records."

"I might do that. What about these three clients you referred to? Lucy mentioned two and gave me one name, Cake?"

"Yeah. Cake. He's a possibility but the cops dismissed him. I think the other one—what was his name—Billy Grubbs, is the more likely suspect. He's a good old boy, a country cracker who has a claim for medical malpractice. He was supposed to get his gall bladder out but they got him mixed up in the hospital with a guy who had prostate cancer. They operated, took out his prostate instead, and cut the nerves so now he can't get it up. Turns out even his gall bladder was okay, he was just lactose intolerant. He isn't a happy man. Anyway, Jack claims there was no case, but it looked solid to me."

"So the guy's been coming around, making threats, what?"

"He was coming by pretty often until Jack was killed. Of course a lot of clients bailed when the news broke. But Grubbs was nobody I would have messed with. He was almost as big as Jack. But I told the cops about him, too. They aren't too interested in looking further when they think they already have their man in custody."

"I'll check it out. What about the third one?"

"No chance. I don't remember her name, but she's a disturbed little old lady who thinks she has a negligence case against the corner convenience store that sold her dead husband hot dogs. He died of a heart attack, you see, and she blames the store for selling them knowing they might raise his cholesterol. There was no legal basis for her complaints against our firm, but she filed against us anyway. I don't see her as a killer. Could have had help though, I suppose."

"One more thing," Oscar said. "How close was Lucy to the inner workings of the firm?"

"Never had any problems with her businesswise. She was the real power behind the office. Chief Paralegal was her title, but she was really in charge of everybody but Jack. She took care of a lot of client contact, helped put together the cases for filing, arranged depositions, handled a lot of correspondence, that sort of thing. She also signed the paychecks from the firm account, so I assume she was involved with the finances. The accountant saw either her or Jack when she came by. So yeah, I'd say she should have had a good hand on the pulse of the office."

"Okay. Your exam is set for one week from Thursday. I'm going to look into a few things before then, talk to some people. Some of the clients might have been involved. I think it also wouldn't hurt to check into both Jack's and Lucy's past. See if there are any ghosts in the closet."

"As far as I'm concerned I did it, Oscar. I told you I'm pleading guilty. Leave it at that and keep Lucy out of it."

"You're not pleading guilty."

Oscar got Roy one more beer and took a pee before he left to become an investigator. He doubted the police would look too closely for other suspects, since they probably closed the investigation with the arrest of Roy. It would be up to him to do the legwork. He considered hiring an outside investigator but hadn't had much luck with them in the past. They were good at using the Internet, interviewing witnesses if you gave them a list. They could do credit and court file checks and followed people real well, but didn't think creatively. Nowadays it seemed most of them relied heavily on computer searches.

Sometimes they even abandoned the job if something better came along. Not a very dependable lot, and most of them didn't stay in the business long once they found out the work wasn't at all like in the Sam Spade books. Sydney did as good a job, worked cheap, and Oscar generally knew where to find her. Plus she was fun to be around.

Chapter Fifteen

Email confirmation of clients sending two second-half payments and one new retainer arrived in the morning along with two seemingly identical requests to burn down two donut shops in suburban Philadelphia. Sydney checked quickly and found the requests came from competing donut makers. She didn't take that kind of job and hit delete.

The new case she had accepted was relatively nearby, in the Pensacola area. It involved a dispute over some badly done engine rebuild work by a marina which resulted in the new client being stranded at sea in his thirty-eight foot Carver Trawler. He unwisely abandoned ship in his tender, and the same marina claimed ten percent salvage rights to the boat when they went out and towed it to port. Maritime law made it legal, but it was just not right. The client was interested in revenge, not getting his money back, so this was right up Sydney's alley. Of course she'd have to take a couple of days off, so with the risk involved the fee was a bit hefty. Even half was worth the job. But how to deal with Rico?

Killing him was not going to be easy. He knew her name, she thought he must have gotten it from Paul at the Pack and Ship, which automatically multiplied the risk to her a thousand fold. Not necessarily the risk of being hurt, but the risk of having his killing pinned on her since she had no idea what records he might have made of their interactions. And he had associates. It seemed likely he was not acting on his own but was the front man for something bigger. Maybe his father's organization. Rico, she had discovered, actually had a law degree but had been unable to get licensed when his misdemeanor convictions were uncovered in the state bar character and fitness investigation. So he worked for dad as a sort of personal assistant—more like an enforcer. Too many layers of difficulty here. So she decided to check out the hit he asked for, maybe do it if it seemed justifiable and thereby rid herself of him. Change her contact information so she was again anonymous. If he found her again she would have no choice but to kill him or disappear. The job he was demanding she do was coincidentally in Apalachicola, not too far from the Pensacola case. Maybe two jobs in one trip. Save on gas.

The problem was collecting the retainer money from now on. Someone had found the mail drop. Probably Rico. The red envelope she picked up had contained nothing but blank paper so it was clearly intended to identify her as the box holder when she came out the door of the shop. She felt safe enough right now, but had to make some changes. Long term, she planned to use wire transfer to an offshore account with an immediate transfer from there to another account. She could have access to that one through a local agent as well as an issued ATM card useable anywhere in the world. But that would have to wait. To do it right she would have go offshore in person.

It took half the day to set up a new mailbox at a private mail service and arrange for the existing one to forward to it. So now the mail would go from New York to Boca Raton before she got it. Paul and Pompano Beach were compromised and unusable now. This business just gets more and more complicated, she thought. Maybe it was time to move on, but she had a thing about Oscar. Love? Well, at least a heavy like and a need to stay around him. She needed him. She knew he needed her too. He just didn't realize it.

Which was why she didn't move out altogether when they broke up. The breakup was her fault. She felt everything was moving too fast toward a conventional life that she wasn't sure she could live. Oscar was sweet about it, even though he was hurt, though she knew he would take her back in a minute. It was actually kind of fun working in the gallery and doing some investigating with him. Like having a family. Something she lost many years ago in the incident that started her Pest Control business. A business that she hoped one day would let her move beyond that horrible time in the past.

Chapter Sixteen

Oscar had expected the meeting with Sheila Katz to take a different turn. He even brought her a fruitcake as a peace offering. Pretty original, he thought. He took pains to wear a tie that matched his suit and two socks the same color.

"Are you trying to bribe me or poison me? What is this? Left over from Christmas?" she said as soon as he set it on her desk.

Oscar guessed that she had quite a few fruitcakes to her credit. Since she refused it, maybe she was one of the people who actually didn't like them?

"No. Not at all, neither. This has nothing to do with any legal matter. This is a gift between fellow attorneys and former friends. A way of trying to patch up our past differences."

"I never really liked you, Leopold, and I still don't. As far as I'm concerned you're attempting to bribe an officer of the court."

She pushed the tin toward him, knocking over in the process two framed pictures of cats that faced her. He caught it as it sailed off the edge of her desk. He liked fruitcake. He would take it home.

"Now what do you want?" She pushed her stringy blond hair out of her eyes so she could glare at him more clearly. When they had dated she seemed ever so much more attractive than she was now. It seemed all the love was lost.

"I wanted to discuss a resolution of my case. Frankly I was surprised any charges were filed at all. It was an obvious case of self-defense, stand your ground, and defense of others. Those guys all had warrants out for them and were assaulting my friend. They threatened me, too."

"Tell that to Mr. Sanchez in the hospital, where he faces the prospect of a knee replacement and possible permanent disability from the gunshot wound you inflicted on him. Any defense you have on the assault charge is far outweighed by your use of unreasonable force. Did you even see any weapons?"

"Now wait a minute, Sheila."

"You can call me Ms. Katz. Do you mind if I record our conversation?" She pulled a small micro-cassette, dictating recorder on the desk and pushed the record button.

"Now. Do you always carry a gun, Leopold? Are you carrying one now?" She reached under her desk where he assumed she either had a gun of her own or a buzzer.

"Of course not. I sometimes keep one in my car for emergency purposes, like the other night, but I bought them legally."

"You don't have a carry permit. You know the law. You used deadly force in a situation that didn't call for it. You can use stand your ground as a defense, but it's my call on filing charges and that's what I did. Now you have to convince the judge like everyone else."

Oscar decided to change direction and let her calm down. A little misdirection might help her gain some perspective.

"Let's talk about Roy for a minute. Is it going to be your file?"

"I authorized the complaint, and I'm the one up, so I think so. I have the file right here. I hope so. Sometimes in a high profile case like this, though, the senior guys fight over it."

"What can you tell me about the case?"

"Only what I'm required by law to tell you. You'll get copies of all witness statements, exculpatory evidence, if any, and witness lists, providing you follow the correct procedures. I haven't decided yet whether to go for the death penalty. I'll let you know."

"Come on, Sheila. Give me a break. Let me look at the file."

She picked up the file, dropped it into a drawer, and slammed it shut. The little recorder fell over.

"What about Roy's alibi? Did you check with Lucy Gamble?"

"Didn't have to. Besides, I have investigators to do that sort of thing. There were other people in the office that night. They were quite certain that Flagler and Lucy weren't there. She's lying for him for some reason. They might have been in on it together.

"Maybe you want to plead him to second degree with the understanding he'll never get parole. You can at least save his life." She looked at her wristwatch, a heavy round man's watch with a black leather band.

"Why don't we start all over like we're total strangers? Let the past stay where it is and deal absolutely professionally with each other?"

"I'll tell you this, Leopold. I have Roy Flagler cold. He killed his boss for revenge and money, plain and simple. He threatened him in public, planned on meeting him at the boat later, and can't account for his time that night. I may not have a smoking gun, but I have more than enough for a jury. I'm going to eat you alive in court if Roy doesn't have enough sense to get another lawyer."

She was spitting just the tiniest bit as she talked. The idea of cooking Roy and Oscar on the judicial platter seemed to be activating her salivary glands. Her face was flushed, and she leaned forward, as if she could hardly wait to get her hands on him.

"What kind of deal can we make on my case?" Oscar was beginning to worry the littlest bit.

"You plead guilty, and I will recommend short prison time. Of course you'll have to give up your law license. Do your clients a favor. You do have a license, don't you?"

Oscar laughed. He reminded himself to send in those overdue bar association dues.

"Really. What can we do? How about I plead no contest to unlawful discharge of a firearm, or disturbing the peace, I pay the fine, you've got a conviction, and we're square."

"I think the conference is over. Don't come see me again. And if I were you I'd get a lawyer. Maybe Roy could represent you." She stood.

He took the fruitcake with him.

Chapter Seventeen

The Toyota was parked in back when Oscar returned to the gallery. The fading yellow front fenders were smeared with greasy hand marks. He couldn't remember washing the car since he had owned it. Usually the heavy rains did the job for him. Since the divorce he lived above the old storefront on a side street just off the main route through the downtown area of West Palm Beach. It was a convenient arrangement, especially in the tourist season when the snowbirds were in town. Oscar enjoyed being able to walk downstairs to work instead of having to fight traffic driving to some office.

He had to devote some time to getting the rest of the show unpacked and hung. He hadn't contacted the printer yet about invitations to the opening, and he needed to send the press release out. His current sculpture was probably drying and shrinking, and he had sent his model out to get a job.

Oscar considered that maybe he shouldn't renew his law license at all. Then maybe he could get some things done. Maybe move to Key West or Miami Beach and open a T-shirt shop. Sounded good in theory, but no doubt that life had its own set of troubles.

He went upstairs and made a cup of coffee, then back down to see how much he had to do to get the show ready. Jesse was nowhere to be seen.

Sydney had unpacked all the paintings. The crates were all stacked in the back room, and she was arranging the paintings around the base of the gallery walls to see which would look best where. She was barefoot and wearing incredibly short cut-off jeans and a stretchy orange tube top with a Harley Davidson bandana wrapped over her head like a skullcap.

The paintings weren't likely to sell to the Palm Beach crowd who liked their artwork in decorator colors. The paintings were abstract acrylics and collage in black, white, and gray. Some had recognizable images, which looked like blow-ups of newspaper and magazine pictures, and words were painted and laminated to the surfaces of the canvas. Dark and foreboding. The society types in their carefully coifed hair sometimes brought in color chips or fabric swatches to match the artwork they were hoping to buy. Oscar lost several sales when he suggested they buy the furniture to match the art rather than the reverse.

"Where's the dog? Outside?"

"I took him to the vet. They're keeping him overnight. Really, Oscar, you have to think about letting him go. In people years he's 119."

"I've had him since I just after I got out of law school. We grew up together. He's my divorce settlement. It's not that easy. Besides, he's happy." Oscar didn't mention that Jesse had been what helped him through the loss of his son years before. The shrink suggested he had transferred his affection to the dog.

"He's embarrassed when he wakes up in a pool of his own urine. The dog is so crippled he can hardly negotiate the one step down to the garden. Get real."

"Jesse's my dog and I'm his owner. I'm all he's got and we aren't giving up until we have to. Anyway, enough about Jesse, he's my problem, I have a mission for you. This time I'll even front some cash."

He thought the word "cash" would Sydney's attention, though he didn't know she had over three-quarters of a million dollars hidden behind a panel in her room. She was working on a way of either laundering it or smuggling it out of the country. She would never have believed that having a lot of money would be such a big problem.

"Do I need weapons for this one?"

"No. At least, I don't think so. I want you to help me check out Lucy and Jack. Their past. I know that she and Jack came from the Apalachicola area, over on the upper Gulf before he opened his office over here a few years ago. We're going over there and find some people they might have known."

"That's near Pensacola isn't it?"

"Not too far. Anyway, I'm particularly interested in how she met him and where he got the money to open the office in West Palm."

"Why don't you just ask her?"

"I intend to. After we get back with the facts. One of the first rules of cross-examination is never asking a question unless you already know the answer." He switched the positions of two of the paintings and stood away from them to see if they were right, then moved them back to where they had been before.

"But this isn't a cross-examination, is it? What's the deal? Do you think she did it?" She had poured the one cup of coffee Oscar made for himself into another cup and was drinking it.

Oscar took the cup away from her.

"I don't know. She had as good a motive as anyone. Lots of insurance money. Possibly more money hidden away that Jack had skimmed from the law practice. I just have to check it out. We'll leave in the A.M."

"Okay with me. I could cover the beach areas. Say, I did some checking on my own. I found out about the guy you shot. Sanchez? He's a bad guy, quite the record. I thought I might go talk to him and see what's up. Maybe he doesn't really want to press charges."

"Stay away from him. I'm handling this myself. Sheila just hasn't made me sweat enough yet. Here," Oscar said, handing her a wad of bills from his pocket, "get the car filled up and the oil changed. See if Angelo can pick up Jesse and watch him till we get back."

"Can we take the Mustang?"

"The Buick. And stick another pistol in the glove box."

Someone was tapping on the gallery window and ringing the bell. Oscar looked over to see that it was obviously a television crew. The cameraman and sound truck were a dead giveaway. He ignored the reporter and his spiked blond hair and walked back into his office, closing the door behind him. At least the gallery was getting some free publicity.

Chapter Eighteen

Oscar hadn't been to Apalachicola in ten years or so. And then he had just driven through on his way from Pensacola. He remembered it from years before as a small fishing village specializing in oyster and shrimp harvesting. The area around it was beginning to change. The Florida building boom was finally spreading to the panhandle area. Unlike the rest of the state, the prime season in the panhandle area was the summer, when tourists from Montgomery and Birmingham used it as an escape from the South's sweltering heat. Pensacola, Gulf Shores, Panama City, all becoming tourist towns. Apalachicola, though, was more of a remote backwater, unaffected so far by most of the commercialism.

Unlike the Southeastern part of the state, the panhandle area's natural vegetation tended more toward pines and oaks than palms. The winter temperatures were cool, with freezing temperature sometimes and highs mostly in the fifties and sixties, keeping the northern tourists farther south. Even so, oystering and fishing was gradually being replaced by tourism as the area's number-one industry.

Sydney said she loved the beach and the ocean but hated the flat landscape of Florida. Oscar pointed out that New York City wasn't exactly mountainous, but Sydney said she believed that all the buildings gave a different impression—a sculptural landscape.

The Florida Turnpike passed through orange groves, ranchland, and most prominently, Orlando and Disney World on its route diagonally across Florida. Development was everywhere, and orange groves had given way to retirement condos, cookie cutter malls, and subdivisions. Compared to Michigan away from the Detroit metro area where Oscar was raised, the terrain was ugly and uninteresting, mostly flat with a few small trees here and there and palmetto swamps dotted around the low areas. With the building boom busted, it wasn't unusual to see half-built subdivisions with skeletal unfinished homes haunting the landscape.

Further north near Ocala they passed through horse country supplying stock for the thriving racing industry. Beautiful country with hundreds of ranches.

US 98 south of Tallahassee was a two-lane blacktop, following the Gulf shoreline, where one slow truck or rubbernecking RV could force you to drive slow and see the sights whether you wanted to or not. The Buick held up pretty well, and they had only had to stop once during the five-hundred-mile trip to have Sydney change a flat tire.

"You know, Oscar, we could make better time if we put the cop lights back on top of the Buick." Sydney was trying to pass the car ahead by driving on the right shoulder. "We could flip them on, and traffic wouldn't be a problem at all."

"What about the little problem of impersonating an emergency vehicle?" Oscar was moving his foot to an imaginary brake pedal as Sydney surged forward and back.

"I got that all figured out. We write 'Volunteer Fire Department' on the sides. Volunteer firemen get to use the lights, right?"

"I'm in enough trouble as it is. Anyway, there's a vacancy sign."

They checked into the Gulf-View Motor Lodge around seven. It was a fading pink single-story stuccoed building with only twelve units across the street from Apalachicola Bay. A small pool was off to one side near a rusting dog pen with no dog, now being used to grow weeds. They were on the edge of town, near the big span of high bridge crossing the river. Shrimp boats with their big net booms extended out from each side like outspread arms could be seen coming in under the bridge with the evening catch. The air smelled like fish, since the docks were upwind of them.

They got the remaining two rooms, a single and a double. Oscar considered briefly telling Sydney there was only one room available, but just as quickly dismissed the idea. She told him a few months ago that she liked girls now. He replied that he liked them, too, not understanding what she was saying. She said no, I mean I *really* like girls. Then he got it. Too many complications. Too much information. Probably just messing with him.

He took the double and borrowed a ragged telephone book from the old man running the desk. He tossed it to Sydney as he got back in the car to pull up in front of the doors to the rooms.

"Here's some research material. And here's your key. We want to find out where Jack worked in town. Get the addresses of the courthouse, the library, newspaper, credit bureau and the law firm with the most names in it. Tomorrow we'll go through some old city directories, if they ever printed any in this place, or old telephone books, and hope Jack and Lucy had a listed number, and find out where they lived. Go to the library, use the Internet, see what you can find."

"I have my IPOD and laptop with me, you know." She lifted the telephone book appraisingly. "I'm surprised you could even find one of these."

"Use whatever you want. Maybe we'll find a coworker, a neighbor, maybe even some family. I'm going to check for public records. They might have owned a house here or got married or something. But for now let's wash up and get some grub over at the Gibson Inn."

The Gibson sat right in the center of town across the long bridge, an old-style wood frame Victorian hotel with two stories, open porches and an in-house restaurant. Oscar automatically had opted for the motel instead of the higher-priced Gibson.

Sydney pulled her luggage, a bright orange gym bag, from the back seat and headed toward her room, fumbling with the key and the telephone book.

"You could have saved money by getting just one room," she said over her shoulder as she smiled, unlocked the door, entered, and closed it behind her.

Oscar stood there trying to figure out whether she meant what he thought she meant, and then decided she was doing a head game number on him and went to his own room to get ready for dinner. He was looking forward to an early night. He was a bit disappointed when at Sydney's knock on the door a while later she just wanted to borrow the car. She was evasive about where she was going and he didn't press it.

Chapter Nineteen

After breakfast they split up. Sydney was quite the sight in her ankle-length white linen caftan with hood. She stayed in town to go through the *Apalachicola Star's* morgue—though it was a weekly and they both hoped the back issues were available. She then was to check the library and the credit bureau, which were all within walking distance of each other. In this town, the commercial area of which was only about six blocks long, everything was in walking distance.

The downtown buildings all looked at least a hundred years old, some even older. It wasn't spruced up and touristy for the most part, though there was a bit of renovation, mostly it was frayed and shabby, waiting for the developers to completely homogenize it. With its two-story brick storefronts and harbor area, it was more New England fishing village than Florida. Victorian wood-frame houses closed in the downtown area on the north and west while the river and gulf covered the other sides. There were a couple of museums celebrating the area's past, and an active riverfront area was still used by the commercial fishermen.

Oscar had made an appointment at ten-thirty with Timothy Bascomb, senior partner of Bascomb, Hughes, & Riner, the oldest law firm in town, according to a clerk at the courthouse. Being a small town it had to have a small legal community. Bascomb would know all the attorneys in the area now or who had ever been in practice here before.

The office was in a large converted wood frame house with a big lawn, surrounding porch and huge overhanging oaks dripping Spanish moss. The central air inside seemed somehow wrong. Oscar thought slow moving ceiling fans and open windows would be more in keeping with the style of the town and the office.

Bascomb kept Oscar waiting in the thickly carpeted and oak paneled reception area for fifteen minutes. He had just finished an intriguing article in *National Geographic* on the dancing bears of the Romanian Gypsies when a male secretary, who reminded Oscar vaguely of a young Robin Williams, showed him to Bascomb's office. He followed the secretary past other attorney-occupied offices and a large data processing room where a half dozen clerks were working diligently in front of computer screens in almost total silence. The furniture and equipment in the place probably cost more than Oscar would earn in a lifetime.

It was twenty steps to Bascomb's desk from the heavy oak door. Bascomb didn't stand when Oscar entered the room. Timothy Bascomb wasn't much older than Oscar's thirty-eight years and, unlike Oscar, still had all his hair. It was thick and blond and somehow annoyed Oscar. Jealousy, he admitted. He had on a dark blue silk suit with one of the little handkerchiefs in the breast pocket that matched his tie. Never saw those anymore. Probably matched his socks and underwear too, thought Oscar.

"Mr. Leopold? I am Timothy Bascomb. How can I help you?" His voice was silky, just like his suit. He had a blank yellow legal pad open in a leather folder in front of him and a gold fountain pen in his left hand. His oversized desk sat in the center of an oriental rug older than the building. A huge crystal chandelier hung in the center of the room from the cypress paneled ceiling.

Oscar shook his hand and sat down without waiting to be asked. Burgundy real leather chairs, nice. He could see the harbor and boats out the large window.

"Nice to meet you. Frankly I expected someone older. Was this a family firm?"

Bascomb smiled. Oscar smiled back.

"My grandfather started the firm. My father died just after I came on board. We do mostly insurance defense and subrogation work." He waited expectantly. Enough small talk Oscar guessed. Time to get to the point.

"I'm defending Roy Flagler. You may have heard he's been charged with the murder of Jack Gamble."

"So you're not a new client?" Bascomb seemed disappointed and dropped the pen onto the pad, his attitude changing from solicitous lawyer to fellow traveler. "Yes. It's been in the newspapers and television. Lawyer killing lawyer. Pretty heady stuff."

"Right now he's the alleged killer. I hope to have some success in the case."

"Of course."

"Did you know Jack Gamble?"

Bascomb leaned back in his chair and steepled his fingers thoughtfully.

"I did know him slightly when he practiced here. It was some time ago. Before he moved east. Before he started advertising."

Oscar sat and waited for him to say more while Bascomb waited for another question. Bascomb gave in first. Some people can't stand more than a few moments of nonconversation.

"We weren't friends or anything like that. He had a small general practice. Marital dissolutions, bankruptcy, drunk driving cases, wills, that kind of thing. I saw him at some of the local bar association functions. I talked to him when he first came to town with a view to asking him to join the firm but after checking him out, decided not to offer him a position."

"Why not?"

"Lack of skill. Lack of credentials. He went to some third-rate law school in Alabama and didn't have good grades even at that. No law review or moot court. No family history. Not our kind of material. And he had no class. Took pride in the fact that his great grandfather was a slave owner. He was a rough-and-tumble sort of character. You know the kind, soup stains on his tie, looked like he slept in his suit."

Oscar tried not to look down at his tie, remembering that he and Roy graduated from what Bascomb would probably consider a second-rate law school.

"How about since then? Since he left here?"

"No. I've never had occasion to see him since he moved east."

"You say you do insurance defense work. Big Jack spent most of his time wringing money out of insurance companies. Did you ever run into him or his firm professionally?"

"I don't personally handle all the litigation cases here. Maybe someone on the staff has had a case with him. I wouldn't know." Bascomb had sat up in his chair now and was fingering the pen again. He glanced at his gold wristwatch. Probably a Rolex, Oscar thought.

"Wouldn't one of your computers be able to give me a list of opposing counsel for the cases your firm has handled lately?" Oscar didn't know what he was fishing for but couldn't help asking. Bascomb seemed a bit evasive and Oscar took that as a sign he was on the right track.

"Maybe. But I see no reason to inquire and no reason to disclose confidential information to you. Particularly when it can have no possible bearing on your case. Anything else I can do for you?"

"Did you know Oscar's wife, Lucy Gamble?"

"Lucy Gamble? Oh, yes. That was a mismatch if I ever saw one. Never understood why she was with him. He was so grotesque and she so, so exotic in a rough sort of way. But women…" he winked, "sometimes find certain things they like about a man that we other men are not privy to."

"What exactly do you mean?" Oscar thought Bascomb was trying to allude to something sexual, perverted or both so decided to call him on it. And he didn't think of Lucy as exotic. Maybe she had changed.

"Never mind. I think we're done now. It was nice meeting you. Be sure to enjoy the beaches out on St. George Island while you're in town Mr.…" he hesitated, "…Leopold. Leonard can give you some nice color brochures of the area and maybe even some discount coupons." He rose, which Oscar took as an invitation to get the hell out, and as if on cue, the door was opened by the secretary, whom Oscar guessed, was Leonard.

As Oscar left, he had to talk fast to make the receptionist understand that he didn't intend to pay for a conference. He thought of having them send a bill to Sheila Katz but decided she didn't need to know where he'd been. A condition of his bond was that he not leave Palm Beach County.

Oscar took off his suit jacket in deference to the heat and the lack of functioning air conditioning in his car, then found a parking place downtown. It took only about three minutes of cruising the few streets to find the courthouse, an old limestone two-story building with few windows a block from the water. It looked more like a nineteenth-century jailhouse from the outside. Finding no shade he parked in the sun and left the windows down. Once inside he tried to find a way of cross referencing cases that Jack might have had opposite Bascomb, Hughes & Riner.

There was a public computer terminal but he couldn't figure out how to use it. After a lot of begging, wheedling, flattery, and insisting, he finally managed to get a clerk to make him a printout of all the court's pending negligence cases, and the attorneys of record. He didn't ask them specifically to give him Bascomb's cases. There were only a dozen attorneys in town, and cooperation might be refused if Bascomb had put out the word on Oscar.

A quick glance through the list showed only one match-up between Gamble's firm and Bascomb's. But these were only the cases actually filed in court. Cases that were being negotiated prior to filing the lawsuit wouldn't be here, and from what he had heard most of Jack's cases never made it to court.

Sydney was stretched out in a reclining deck chair by the pool when Oscar got back to the hotel. He couldn't tell through the mirrored sunglasses if she was sleeping. The pool had no water in it, and weeds peeked through cracks in the concrete patio. He thought that the red top of Sydney's little bikini clashed with the bright green bottom. Those colors only seemed to work together at Christmas. Just like orange and black for Halloween.

"The ozone layer is disappearing you know. You're just asking for skin cancer lying out here in the sun like that."

"Thanks, Dad." Sydney didn't move.

Oscar felt embarrassed standing over her like an aggressive voyeur, though he had seen every inch of her at one time or another. So he pulled over one of the lounge chairs that looked least likely to collapse, and sat next to her.

"What did you find out?"

She sat up, pulled the sunglasses up to her forehead, squinted at the bright sun, and then dropped them back down.

"I found out a lot. Mostly from the lady running the newspaper. It seems that Lucy Gamble, formerly Lucy Harris, was Jack's client before she was Mrs. Gamble."

"And?"

"And her first husband, Robert, was killed in an accident. Big Jack represented her, sued, and collected a huge settlement. The papers didn't say how much, but checking with some of the people at the paper, and at the marina, I found out it was in the neighborhood of five hundred thousand."

"Nice neighborhood."

"So they say. Then, just after that Lucy and Jack were married in the local courthouse and moved away."

"So that's where Jack got the money to open the Palm Beach office." He knew that Jack Gamble had started out big time when he came to Palm Beach from Apalachicola. He had leased an entire building on Australian Avenue, hired a staff, equipped the office, and started an advertising blitz. That took big bucks.

"And guess what kind of accident Lucy's husband died in."

"Okay, what?"

She grinned, picked up the can of Budweiser from under her chair and took a sip. "A boat explosion."

Back at the courthouse it took only a few minutes to locate the file of The Estate of Robert Harris vs. Gulfcraft Yacht Sales, et al. The case had been filed alleging general acts of negligence, nothing specific. He was surprised at the small size of the file. On the surface it appeared to be in order, and legally sufficient, but there were only the barest minimum of depositions and other discovery taken. Oscar could think of a half dozen affirmative defenses and motions to dismiss that weren't raised by the defense. No jury trial was asked for by either side, and it settled only three months from the filing date.

He knew that the defense of nearly all negligence cases was paid for by the defendant's insurance company. No insurance usually meant no deep pocket to dip a settlement from. I was not surprising then, since the biggest insurance defense firm in town was Bascomb, Hughes & Riner, that Timothy Bascomb was the attorney of record. He thought he should discuss this with Mr. Bascomb, so he telephoned. The receptionist came back on the line after a minute, and said Mr. Bascomb was gone for the day.

Oscar went back to Bascomb's office. The receptionist immediately buzzed someone when Oscar walked in and whispered something before he could get up to her desk. Oscar saw Leonard peering around the corner at him and waved to him. Leonard almost smiled, waved back automatically, then ducked out of sight.

"Can I help you?" The receptionist showed Oscar her nice teeth.

"Mr. Bascomb please. He was here a just a while ago. I just have one short question for him. It won't take much time. I promise."

"He's gone for the day. Were you the one who called?"

"Yes. But I don't have to see him. Maybe one of the other partners?"

"Just a moment. Why don't you take a seat? Your name?"

"Leopold. Oscar Leopold. It hasn't changed since I saw you two hours ago. I had on a suit jacket then, and still have the stain on my tie." He held the tie up for her to see.

He sat down, and picked up the same issue of *National Geographic*. He had always meant to subscribe since it seemed to be such a privilege. It used to be you didn't really subscribe as such, but were invited to become a member of the society, which entitled you to the magazine. He was wondering if he would be invited to go on one of their expeditions if he joined, when Bascomb came out, carrying a briefcase. He had his car keys in his hand.

"I'm in a hurry Leopold. What do you want now?"

He stood. "I just found out that you were the defense attorney in the Lucy Harris wrongful death case a few years ago."

Bascomb looked at his watch.

"You remember? Lucy Harris, now known as Lucy Gamble, wife of the late Robert Harris and the late Jack Gamble?"

"Yes. I remember now. It slipped my mind. So what?"

"Well, doesn't it strike you as a little too coincidental that both of Lucy's husbands died in boat explosions?"

"We live near the Gulf. People have boats. Accidents happen."

"But Big Jack's death wasn't an accident."

"I wouldn't know about that. And I don't see what possible relevance my involvement in the old case could have to your defense of Jack's alleged killer. Perhaps you should take your suspicions to the police." He tried to step past Oscar but Oscar didn't move.

"Do you always do the same kind of Cracker-Jack defense for all your clients that you did on Lucy's case? Or have you gotten more skillful as time has passed?"

Bascomb reddened. Oscar hoped to provoke some sort of reaction that Bascomb had not had time to carefully think out.

"I have no more time for this," he said in a studied, even-toned, jaw-clenched manner. "We have the most respected law firm in this part of the state. I don't need some third-rate hack questioning my abilities."

"I try to think of myself as a first-rate hack, but it's just that the case settled so quickly, and for so much money. I didn't even see much liability there. Did you and Jack have some kind of special understanding?"

"Get out of this office!" He had raised his voice now. "Call the sheriff," he said over his shoulder to the receptionist. She immediately picked up the telephone receiver. "Tell them we have a trespasser."

"Okay. Calm down," Oscar said. "No reason to lose your temper." He knew from dealing with his ex-wife that angry people hate to be told to calm down. "I'm leaving voluntarily. No need for the police."

The police were the last thing he needed in his current legal situation. He noticed that Bascomb didn't follow him out, though he had said he had to leave. On a whim Oscar pulled out of the lot then parked in the shade in the Gibson Inn parking lot across the street from Bascomb's building. After fifteen minutes he was about to leave when he saw Bascomb walking in a hurry toward his car. No briefcase. The only white Jaguar in the lot was his, and he pulled out into traffic without slowing, causing an oncoming motorcycle to swerve around him to avoid a collision.

Oscar made a U-turn in the street and followed. He was no expert at tailing anyone, but rather enjoyed the experience. If he remembered the procedure from the days when he watched television police dramas, he was supposed to stay one or two cars back to avoid being spotted. The method worked great as they passed out of town and onto the bridge heading east. Just over the bridge Bascomb turned right on a narrow road with a real estate office on the corner, following a sign to St. George Island.

Oscar pulled over, let a pickup get between him and the Jag, and followed as they passed through a green tunnel of several hundred yards of overhanging trees, then came out into brilliant sunshine and started over a causeway leading straight out into the Gulf of Mexico. On the horizon in the ocean several miles ahead, Oscar could see a long low island paralleling the shoreline. The two lanes of traffic whizzed by in opposite directions, missing each other by inches, seemingly defying the odds of multiple head-on collisions. Cars were pulled off the road here and there, and groups of people sat in lawn chairs or on the seawall fishing.

A man standing in his boat near the causeway was emptying a long handled rake full of oysters onto a pile in the middle of his boat. Several other oystermen were visible across the bay, their yellow rubber boots dotted color across the choppy water.

Finally over the bridge, they entered the island. It was only a few hundred yards wide, but appeared to be miles long, more of a big sand bar than anything else. There was little commercial activity, just a few beachside restaurants, a bar, two gas station/convenience stores, a bait shop, and a couple of beachwear tourist stores. Young people walked barefoot up and down the streets wearing as little as legally allowed.

The car turned right, and Oscar followed past rows of beach houses built on stilts, either for higher than normal tides or possibly just for a better view of the water. Many had 'for rent' signs in front of them. A lot more were for sale. Some of the owners bought the houses strictly for investment, letting them out at indecent weekly rents to northern tourists when they could. Speculators had dumped a lot of money in the island real estate and Oscar had read that the foreclosure rate was high.

He was glancing at the gulf and its dazzling white sand beaches, and at the college kids playing volleyball as he drove along, so wasn't ready when the car ahead stopped unexpectedly for pedestrians. Drivers were not so polite in West Palm and would have veered around them rather than stopping. Oscar stomped on the brake pedal, and the Buick skidded sideways on the sand covered roadway, leaving a black smoking skid of burned rubber on the pavement. The driver ahead saw in his mirror what was happening, and shot ahead to avoid getting hit, avoiding the pedestrians and a rear end collision but instead ramming into a telephone truck making a left turn from the corner. Oscar pulled around them, avoiding the broken glass, hoping to catch up with Bascomb.

Up ahead the road ended. That is, the public traffic was diverted left and right. A guardhouse and striped wooden barrier arm blocked the road straight ahead into a compound called The Plantation. The rear end of the Jaguar was disappearing around the curved drive bordered by tropical landscaping as Oscar pulled up.

The gray-haired heavyset security guard leaned out his window, smiling. He had on a short sleeved blue cop type shirt with gold patches on the shoulders reading Guardall Security.

"Can I help you, sir?"

"Yes. I'm with Mr. Bascomb. He just went through." Oscar removed his sunglasses and tried to give a convincing grin.

"He didn't say anything about you." The guard pulled down a clipboard and flipped through several pages.

"No. I was supposed to be right behind him and follow him in, but he got ahead. You can call if you want, but it's okay. I can pull over and wait. He'll just be one drink ahead of me by the time I get there."

The gate raised as the guard pushed a hidden button.

"No. That's alright. It looked like you were following him to me. Go on ahead and take this pass." He handed over a white paper rear view mirror tag with the date written in black marker.

Oscar drove on in, hoping he could find the house. He couldn't very well ask the guard for the address.

The end of the island comprising The Plantation was heavily forested with pines and palms, and neatly landscaped, unlike the open sandiness Oscar had just left. The houses were mansions really, huge architectural marvels hidden on private drives off the main road that had no buildings fronting it. The ocean wasn't visible at all, though Oscar could hear the surf to his left through his open window.

Just past the next intersection he spotted the Jaguar pulling into a condominium complex. He slowed, and circled the block, entering the same driveway a few minutes later. The car was parked in front of a white three-story glass and stone building with a red tile roof of the kind the rich and famous own in the movies. Tall silver-trunked nonindigenous royal palm trees had been planted artfully around the property. Bascomb was outside in a small courtyard hugging a beautiful brunette woman wearing shorts and a halter top. Two children, a boy about six, and a girl a year or so older, were riding bicycles around a small concrete fountain on the pavers near the front door. Quite a domestic scene.

Oscar drove back to the motel after writing down the address.

Sydney wasn't answering her door when he got there so he picked up a copy of the *Pensacola Times*, page one featuring an explosion and fire the night before at the local public marina. A lot of that going around lately.

The next morning they were to head back home, but when Oscar got up the car was gone and so was Sydney. A note stuck in his door said cryptically "I'll be back. Stay there." A box of a half dozen donuts and a cold cup of coffee were on the chair sitting outside the door.

Chapter Twenty

From his high-backed rocking chair on the wide-planked wooden porch of the Gibson Inn, Rico watched the parking lot of the office building across the street while petting one of the Inn's big yellow cats. A rumpled gym bag was on the chair next to him. Rico had checked into the Gibson earlier that day, waiting for Sydney to appear. He had hired her to do the hit that was supposed to happen yesterday but didn't, and he was a bit concerned she wouldn't follow through. The job was too important to leave to chance. It looked like she wasn't going to show today either.

It was late afternoon. The offices would be closing soon, and Rico watched to see if Bascomb stayed late or if he would have to follow him. The white Jaguar sedan was still in the lot along with a half-dozen other cars. Rico fanned himself with the Miami paper he had managed to locate at the local CVS Pharmacy and rocked, not taking his eyes off the building across the street. He was annoyed at having to be here at all. Can't seem to get reliable help nowadays, he thought. He had brought his girlfriend Carmen with him as cover, whom they had agreed would be called Gloria for this trip. A lone man with no apparent purpose in town might be noticed, while a couple would be written off as tourists.

"Rico?" Gloria asked.

"I told you to call me Tony this week," Rico replied, not looking at her.

"Tony? How come we have to stay at the hotel all day? I wanted to go to the beach."

"I told you to look around town. It's historic, a fishing village, people come from all over to see this corner of Florida."

"I did that. After you see the fish market and the arts & craft shops, that's about it. They don't even have cable in the room. Or even a TV."

"I told you, it's historic. You pay extra for no TV." Rico stopped rocking. People were coming out of the building now, getting into their cars. "I tell you what," he said, turning to her. She was hugging the fat cat. Now she'd have cat hair all over her. Rico had always hated cats, especially after his mother had accused him of killing theirs. Sure, he'd done it, but the neighbor kids were in on it too.

"How about if we go over to the beach on the island for dinner after we're done here? I got us a reservation for seven-thirty at that oyster bar place we saw yesterday."

"You are the best." She said, putting the cat down gently as she leaned over and kissed him on the cheek.

When only the Jaguar remained in the parking lot, Rico sent Gloria inside and walked across the lawn and street to the office building, taking the gym bag with him. He slipped a small pill in his mouth and chewed it on the way.

Timothy Bascomb was waiting for a telephone call. He had been shaken after the visits from that Oscar Leopold. He was likely to find out something and seemed to suspect Bascomb's role in it. R.J. Walters wasn't returning his calls, and he didn't know what to do next. A scandal like this might not be a problem in a big metropolitan area, but in a small town he would be disgraced and ruined.

Bascomb finally sent a text message. *Call me now or I'll do whatever I have to do to protect myself.* Still no call, even with the threat. Didn't they realize he could send them all to jail? He had contacts with the State's Attorney's office and a lot of inherited influence that he would use if the cover blew off this thing. Them or me, he thought. And it won't be me. He leaned back in the leather executive desk chair, coat off, tie loosened, and eyes closed, trying to will away the headache.

He heard the front door buzzer, surprised, thinking everyone had already left. Hadn't they locked the door? Sometimes clients stopped in unannounced, but now there was no office staff to act as gatekeeper. He would have to attend to it.

He stood, buttoned his shirt collar, and slipped his tie back in place. Had to look right. Bascomb was not one of those Florida lawyers who opted for short sleeves and no suit jacket in deference to the heat. He was halfway to his office door when Rico stepped through, stopped, and just stood there. His Orlando Magic baseball cap nearly touched the top of the doorway. The Hawaiian shirt and designer sunglasses made him out a tourist—not the type of outfit worn by the locals. In his left hand was a gym bag, from which he now removed a large handgun, showed it to Bascomb and put it back.

"What do you want? We only keep petty cash here, but I have a few hundred dollars and credit cards on me." He had never been threatened with a gun or robbed. His legs were suddenly shaky, and he could actually feel his heart thumping. He told himself it was probably nothing. Maybe just one of the local rednecks with a complaint. And it seemed everybody had a gun permit these days.

"Relax, Mr. Bascomb. I don't want your money."

"I already called the sheriff. They'll be here any minute. Why do you have a gun if it's not a robbery?"

"No. You didn't call and it's not a robbery. This is a suicide." Rico pulled a coiled length of blue rope from the bag and held it out to Bascomb. "I found this last night tied to your boat on the trailer outside your garage. You were having dinner with the wife and kids. I didn't want to bother you. "

"What the hell are you talking about? You're going to kill yourself here? And how could you get to my boat? I live in a gated community. We have security."

"No. I'm not the one. The suicide would be you. Here's the deal. You'll take this rope, tie it to that fixture there," he pointed to the heavy antique chandelier hanging in the center of the room. "Then, you stand on one of those fancy leather chairs, tie the rope around your neck and tip the chair over. Pretty simple, isn't it? Even a lawyer could follow those directions."

"This is preposterous. I will do no such thing. Go ahead and shoot me, but I won't do the job for you." Bascomb felt his chest tightening. His knees buckled slightly. The adrenaline surging through his system made him light-headed. He thought of running, but the man stood between him and the door and there was no rear entrance. He could lock himself in the bathroom if he could get to it, but there was the gun. His cell phone was in his desk and out of reach. The burglar alarm panic button was on his key chain—also in his desk.

"Yes. You will. Here, sit down a minute, we'll talk and you'll understand. You look white as that famous sugar sand beach you people talk about so much. Now take one of those chairs from in front of the desk and slide it over there, under the chandelier."

Bascomb hesitated, but did it.

"Now would be a good time to have a seat."

Bascomb dropped into the chair, his hands gripping the chair arms tightly, looking around the room for anything that might help, still thinking of possible escape.

"Here, take a look at these pictures." He pulled his cell out of his pocket, pushed a button and turned it so Bascomb could see the picture. "That's your wife Catherine with Lisa and Matthew out in front of the house, isn't it?"

Bascomb felt like he had been slammed in the chest. The guy knew where he lived—had been there. Had somehow bypassed security and watched them at the house. He knew the names of the children.

"You see, Timothy, if you refuse, I have a lot of options. I may shoot your wife. Maybe rape her first in front of your kids. Then kill them, too. Or maybe the other way around. Rape the kids while one or both of you watch. Throw in a little torture.

Then I might even let you live, but as a paraplegic. Lots of bad things could happen that you can prevent real easy. And you know I know how to get at them. And we both know you're not an innocent—you have things to atone for. This can save a lot of embarrassment for you if things keep going the way they are.

"At best, it's all going to work out badly for you no matter what happens. But you can stop the exceptionally bad and painful things from happening to your wife and kids by following instructions. You have the power to save them. It's up to you. To the police, when it's all over, it's either going to look like your tragic suicide, or worse, if you don't cooperate, a mass murder by someone else. Messy. I know you want to do the right thing. So what'll it be?"

Rico was jumpy, shifting his weight from foot to foot and talking fast as he stood over Bascomb. Bascomb considered lunging at him, maybe shoving him aside to get out the door. But knew his own limitations. This wasn't Bascomb's arena. He could squash anyone in a court room. Words were his weapons. He was powerless here and truly believed the man would do as he threatened. The gun was irrelevant given the size of this guy. There was no choice. He thought about his wife and the children. Tears welled in his eyes. Maybe someone would walk in, or the phone would ring and distract him.

"Who sent you?" he asked, his voice trembling, trying to stall for time, his eyes darting around the room, hoping for some miracle, some kind of help. But while he knew anything could happen, that there was always a chance, most of the time things just proceed on their own and happen as planned without any intervening fortuitous event.

"I think you know why I'm here. There's no chance we're going to let you roll over for the police and destroy all we've worked for. You got your share, just like we did. Just take the rope. Make it easy on yourself. You know it's going to happen." He held it out again.

Bascomb hesitated, wearily stood up, and then accepted the rope, thinking resignedly about how his wife might handle the kids' college tuition one day. Would the life insurance pay off?

"One thing," Bascomb asked, gripping the rope tightly with both hands. "Could I use the bathroom? I mean, I don't want…"

"Afraid of shitting yourself? I bet you read that in a book. Actually I've seen it happen a few times. It's when the sphincter relaxes at death, but don't worry about it. You won't be alive to feel any embarrassment."

Bascomb was twirling in a slow circle under the chandelier when the door buzzer went off the second time. Rico had waited until the strangling rope did its job and now reached for the gym bag and the gun, not knowing who had come in.

Sydney came through the office door and crouched in a military firing stance, feet apart and both hands holding what looked to Rico like an old Army .45 aimed directly at the center of his chest.

"You. On the ground, on your face now," she said, gesturing with the gun.

Rico smiled as he reached to pull the gym bag to him.

"Leave it."

"Big gun for a little girl. You must be Sydney."

"And you must be Rico." Her mind was racing.

"So it looks like you're too late to do what I paid you for. I decided time was of the essence and didn't know how reliable you were. You still owe me one."

"No. We're even if I decide to let you live and definitely even if I don't."

Rico glanced at the bag on the floor, but the .45 precluded going for it.

Sydney moved a few feet to the right of the doorway to leave room for Rico to exit and still have a safe margin to shoot him if necessary.

"Now I want you to walk across the parking lot and up the street until I can't see you anymore. I am an excellent shot, so don't look back and don't think about trying to follow me or contact me again. You don't want to be my next target."

"No problem. But I might have more work for you in the future. Can I get you through your website?"

"I'm out of business. Goodbye."

"I've got to say I admire your nerve. Your hands are rock steady. Most women couldn't do what you do."

"Yeah, I'm terrific. Now go."

Sydney considered shooting him right there. He deserved it. But she had no idea who else was around, whom he had come with. And there was only one practical way out of town for her over the mile-long bridge. The earlier research for Oscar had turned up quite a lot on Bascomb too. Often accused, never charged. A big firm in a small venue that got away with whatever they wanted. The local judge had been a partner in the firm at one time, so they were insulated. Not enough bad news for her to kill him, but apparently Rico's associates had a lower threshold than her or more at stake. She had been surveilling Bascomb when she saw Rico go in. She knew it was him. Looked just like his picture she found from her earlier research. No suit this time. Saving Bascomb, as sleazy as he was, had entered her mind, but then what? Too many crumbs to sweep up. Walking away was probably the best option, but she needed closure with this guy. There was no time to call the police, and when she finally decided to intervene it was too late.

Rico stood for a minute, then just turned and walked away as instructed, leaving the gym bag. When he finally got back to the hotel he stayed away from the office building, packed up Gloria and left town. No dinner on the beach. Sydney had looked at the crime scene, picked up Rico's bag, decided Bascomb would be accepted as a suicide, and left through the rear door.

Chapter Twenty-one

They left early the following morning to get back to West Palm during daylight. She had no explanation other than "personal business" for being gone the day before. Oscar pressed a bit; she wouldn't talk. Oscar briefed her on the Bascomb meeting on the way. She was unusually quiet. He was glad she had come along, even though it delayed their trip a day. He had a chance to relax for the first time in weeks. He hated long drives and would usually make what could be a one-day trip into two just because he disliked the travel tedium so much. With Sydney doing the driving, and having her to talk to, Oscar could tolerate it. Flying had been his other option, but he would have had to rent a car when he arrived, and not having any credit cards made such a transaction difficult. He hadn't cashed the check that Roy had sent him yet, so he was down to a couple of hundred dollars in cash when they got back to town.

The engine of the Buick was knocking loudly and smoking when they pulled in behind the gallery. It continued to run for a minute or so after Sydney shut it off, then finally rattled, farted, and died. She jumped on her motorcycle and took off, and Oscar decided he should look up Roy again. He wanted to see if this new information about Lucy would be a revelation to him.

Wednesday morning he tried to call Roy but he didn't answer, but Oscar figured he might be eluding the press. He would stop by his house later. There were sixteen messages on voice-mail. After listening to the first few and finding that they were all from news people, he deleted them all.

He needed to eat, thought over his choices, ruled out the Ebb Tide, and decided on a quick hamburger and beer at Smokey Joe's since it was on the way to Roy's.

Following Lucy had been easy for Rico. The hard part would be getting her alone so he could ask a few questions. She lived in a gated community, and Rico wanted his visit to be anonymous. No witnesses. Not that he intended to get physical, but sometimes people just wouldn't listen to reason and open up to him. His previous attempt at getting to her at the restaurant had ended badly and he had been unable to get to her at home. So he had followed her here. He needed the information that she must have that they had been unable to get from Jack Gamble. And then there was the money that Jack must have stashed. R.J. may not care about it, but Rico saw a potential bonus if he got Lucy's cooperation, willing or otherwise.

She drove up to a garage in what Rico considered a boring middle-class subdivision, not gated. The garage door opened, and then closed behind her car as she drove in and parked next to another car. He knew this wasn't her house. She had a boat, if you called a forty-seven-foot Hatteras yacht a boat, that he had followed her to but the marina had been crowded. Then there was the condo down on the Intracoastal, but it had heavy security with fences, a guard house and cameras very evident. This garage belonged to the house where the lawyer Roy Flagler lived. Rico had dossiers on all the principals involved in the insurance scheme, but he had never been to this address. He knew Roy lived alone. Interesting that she had a garage door opener to his house. So they must be there alone and together.

Rico waited ten minutes to see if she stayed, then pulled into the driveway, parking the van in front of the garage door, nonchalant, like he belonged. He knew that some neighbors in subdivisions monitored all activity in and out, and didn't want to raise suspicions with the Neighborhood Watch. The white van would be a good disguise since all the maintenance and service people drove them. No one came out of the house or pulled aside any curtains as he sat and waited. He checked the front door. Locked. He didn't use the doorbell, but walked around the garage across the grass to the rear of the house. The screened door to the Florida room was also locked, but not after Rico cut the nylon screening and reached inside. The sliding glass door to the family room was open.

No one was in sight. He kept his knife out, holding it casually to his side as he slipped inside and stood listening.

There was a van in Roy's driveway that Oscar didn't recognize. A big work van. Maybe a contractor of some kind, he thought. Or an air-conditioning man. Oscar noticed when he drove down the street that his ex-wife Pam's house had a new black Mercedes parked in the driveway. She seemed to be coping well with the divorce. He remembered buying the house with her. They had it built from standard plans but got to pick out the carpeting, tile, cabinets, and light fixtures. It had cost a bundle to furnish. The only new house he had over bought.

They picked out the neighborhood because there were other young couples with children and—he stopped himself, remembering too much, and hoped she didn't notice him driving by. All too often she wanted to drop in when he was visiting Roy on one pretext or another. Oscar had no desire to see her, consciously trying to erase that chapter from his past. The past was just memories, and he wanted none of them related to her. She treated him condescendingly, as if he were damaged goods. Thank God for Sydney, who would likely just tell him to suck it up, be a man. He needed that.

Oscar parked in the street in front of Roy's, tried the doorbell, waited, then went around the side through the grass that needed mowing, and past the shrubbery that needed trimming, and went in through the Florida room, not noticing the cut screen. He helped himself to a beer, thinking that since he might be in jail soon he had to enjoy freedom while he could, and called out, "Hey, Roy! Are you home or what?"

No answer. But he heard sounds coming from upstairs. Music and some sort of a shuffling noise, like someone was trying to crawl into a closet. The back door had been unlocked. Roy hadn't opted for the security system that was available with the houses in the subdivision, choosing instead to buy decals and a yard sign that warned of a monitored alarm system. But he didn't buy the system itself, just the signs. Roy could be napping or it may be an intruder. What was with the van? Either way Oscar decided to check it out quietly. He started carefully up the stairs. Soft classical music was coming from one of the rooms.

The master suite, a bathroom, and three other bedrooms led off the sitting room from the landing. He moved quietly on the carpeted floor. The first two small bedrooms were empty. The music was louder near the master suite. Oscar pushed the master suite door open with his foot, and stood back as it swung open. No creaky hinges.

Roy was on his knees in the middle of the king-size bed, naked, face flushed, almost a grimace on his face, sweating, and behind Lucy, his hands on her hips, his big hairy belly resting on her upraised buttocks. She was just as naked in front of him on her hands and knees; her breasts and long red hair hanging down and swinging back and forth with his thrusts. They were both facing him, and she screamed as she pulled away from Roy and jumped to her feet on the other side of the bed, leaving Roy still on his knees, not knowing what to do. She wasn't a true redhead Oscar noted, and didn't look very exotic at the moment.

There are some sights Oscar wished he had never seen, scenes that are never erased from the memory banks. This one of Roy now topped his list.

He went back downstairs with a short, "Oops, sorry," drank down the beer, and opened another.

"Goddamn it, Oscar!" Roy said as he stomped down the stairs. Oscar hoped he wasn't planning on hitting him. Roy was pulling the belt tight on his silk bathrobe, and was barefoot.

"This is my house, my bedroom, and I damn well expect that it should be private. I should sue your ass."

"Get in line." Oscar couldn't help but laugh then. "Listen, I really am sorry. I had no idea. I thought there was a burglar. Really. There's a van." He tried not to laugh again. Roy didn't share the humorous nature of the situation.

"Well, what about Lucy?" He went for the refrigerator instead of Oscar's throat. Oscar had the last beer in his hand. He handed it quickly to Roy. "How's she going to face you again?" Roy drained the can in one big gulp.

"I'm a big girl, Roy." Lucy stepped down the stairs in a white terry robe that came just below her crotch. Her bare legs were nicely tanned, and her toenails were painted bright pink. She had pinned her hair up, and her makeup was noticeably smeared.

"And Oscar knows all about sex. Don't you Oscar? It was just a mistake. No big deal." She pulled a pack of cigarettes and a blue Bic lighter from the pocket of the robe and lit one. Very cool.

"It's a big deal to me," Roy said, calming down. He sat on one of the four wicker bar stools surrounding the butcher block island in the kitchen.

"What about the van in the driveway," Oscar asked.

"That's mine," said Rico, walking down from upstairs.

"Who the hell are you?" demanded Roy. He looked at Rico then at Lucy, who appeared to be deciding whether to scream.

"You messed up the free show for me," he said, pointing the knife at Oscar. He circled the island, and patted Oscar down lightly for weapons. He stood back, his weight on the balls of his feet watching all of them.

"I know you two aren't carrying," he said to Roy and Lucy, not smiling, "but I ought to check you closer, honey," he said to Lucy. "Maybe in a few minutes upstairs."

Lucy swallowed and blinked, trying to maintain her composure, the aloof hardness gone now. To her credit she looked him right in the eye and blew smoke at him, but said nothing.

"Who are you, and what do you want?" Oscar asked. He was startled by this stranger walking in, and didn't know quite how to react. Roy was just staring open-mouthed at the man.

"You can call me Rico, and I just need a few answers. And since you're all here, you save me a lot of time questioning you one at a time. What I want is for you all to cooperate. I need information on Jack Gamble, and some business he had with my boss. Now I know that if that information is out there, one of you has it or can get it."

"So what's the information?" Roy asked. His voice sounded strangled. His sweating was worse than ever, and his robe had fallen open exposing his hairy, protruding belly. The upstairs vision entered Oscar's head again.

"Mr. Gamble had some computer lists of certain transactions between his firm and mine. Walters, Schaefer, and Gregg. This was financial stuff, mostly data concerning private investment deals between the two of us. Legal cases we were both involved in that I can't have made public. It's got no value to any of you but is important to my associates. And to me. So I want it. And you're going to give it to me or my next visit will have an unhappy ending. You should look for a computer disk or flash drive that he may have hidden. Maybe even a printout. Look in his private safe deposit box or home safe. Anywhere he might hide important stuff."

"We don't know what you're talking about," Lucy said, her voice restored now that it looked like the immediate danger was past. "I was his wife and office manager. If he had anything like that, I would know. And if you really are a lawyer what's with the strong-arm stuff?"

"The death took you hard, huh? Looks like you found a way to deal with it. My kind of woman. And to answer your question I don't have time to wait for the legal process. I find self-help is often the best help. I need the data and I have to be certain there are no copies. If I find out there were—well let's just say you will all regret it." Rico nearly smiled.

"Go to hell," said Lucy.

"I am 99 percent sure that you, and maybe all of you, already have what I want or know where it is. So I'll give you time, but not much. To be sure of your cooperation I want one of you to come with me until the others produce. Guess which one I'm taking." He smiled, then looked at Lucy.

Oscar looked around the kitchen. The guy seemed to just have the knife, but that was more than they had in the way of weapons. On the one hand he was outnumbered; on the other they were unarmed, and who knew how skilled he might be with that thing. Sometimes, though, fortuitous things just happen. On the other hand, bad things could be just as likely. Most of the time, nothing happened, the events just played themselves out. This time they were lucky.

The doorbell rang.

Looking through the living room across the foyer they could see someone cupping their hands around their face close to the glass, trying to look in through the sheer drapery in the window next to the door. It was a woman. She called out,

"Oscar? I saw your car. Can you hear me?" The doorbell rang again.

Oscar considered answering, but a look at Rico kept him quiet. Lucy started to speak, but Rico grabbed her arm roughly.

It was Oscar's ex-wife, Pam. One of the few times he was glad to see her. Maybe she was finally going to do him some good, Oscar thought.

They watched quietly and saw her move away from the door, then cross the window, across the lawn toward the side of the house toward the rear door.

"Okay. I'm going now, a little earlier than planned, but remember what I said. Find the info I want, and find it soon. It'll be in the best interest of your personal health. Next time it won't be so much fun." He let go of Lucy, and went out the front door, closing it quietly.

Oscar went to the door and watched the van pull away but couldn't get the license number. There was no plate. Pam had heard the van start and come back to the front of the house. Oscar talked to her for a minute and then sent her home, coming back inside.

Roy had given up on the beer, and was mixing vodka martinis for the three of them. Lucy was looking through the telephone book with the telephone receiver in her hand, saying, "Police, police, where the fuck is the number?" Oscar took the phone from her, hung it up, and closed the book.

"Did you ever hear of 911?" he asked. "Anyway, we don't need the police on this. Roy and I have enough police problems right now. This guy is with the Walters firm, and we all know who he is. The question is what was he talking about?"

Lucy shrugged. Roy looked at her, and lifted his hands palms up. "Beats me," he said. "Must be some private deal with Jack. Maybe somebody else he screwed over."

Lucy looked at him, a hurt look on her face.

"Sorry, just a gut feeling based on my own past relationship with the man."

"Speaking of relationships, what is this with you two?" Oscar asked. "Has this been going on long?"

Roy looked at Lucy. She replied. "A while. Since before Jack's death. And since then Roy has been helping me with taking care of Jack's estate."

"I know this might be an inopportune time, Lucy, but could I ask you a few questions about Jack?" He decided to wait, and ask her privately about Apalachicola.

"You can ask. I'll decide if I want to answer."

"Tell me about Jack's money."

"Money? You mean Jack's supposed stash that he had put away? I don't know where it is, if it exists at all."

"You were his wife. And worked with him. You had to be in on most of the information."

"Look." She tossed her cigarette into the sink. It sizzled, and went out when it hit the wet surface. Smoke came out of her mouth as she talked. "I know Jack was involved in something. Some kind of inside deal with some other lawyers. He brought in tons of money. A lot more than I thought he should be able to on the cases we had. It was like he never had a loser. Big money, policy maximums on every case. But there was never any cash in the firm. He said his investments didn't pan out. And our personal accounts don't show it. If it wasn't for the life insurance, I'd be screwed." She smiled then, and patted Roy's shoulder.

"I don't buy that," Oscar said. "A firm that size has big time accountants and tax people. He didn't operate it out of the check book in his back pocket. There have to be records."

"There were. In Jack's office. We had two separate accounts. He deposited everything in his account and just transferred whatever I told him we needed to cover the office expenses. He never let anybody see his records. It was all on the office computer, but he was the only one who had the password to his private files."

"What about your personal taxes? You had to sign the returns."

"He didn't show much income. At least not the kind I thought he was making. And the firm had its own tax number. He took care of that himself. He was just an employee he told me. I hope to hell there's money somewhere, and that I can find it."

"Oscar," Roy said, "I didn't know anything about Jack hiding money, if that's what he was doing. My cases went just like they always did. I won and lost my share at trial and settled a fair number. But Jack always settled, never went to trial and settled very well. I can tell you something that I thought was unusual, though. He insisted on personally handling all cases that had certain defense firms working on the other side. He said he had a special relationship with them. I think I can speculate now on what that relationship might have been."

"Like Walters' firm, for example?"

"That's one example."

"And Bascomb, Hughes, & Riner?"

"That's another. How did you know that?"

"You think there was some money changing hands under the table?"

"I don't know. I can't prove it. But it sounds plausible."

"So why plead guilty?" Oscar asked, "You say you were with Lucy. With an alibi they might never have filed charges at all."

"You're pleading guilty?" Lucy asked.

"I'll talk to you about this later. Go on upstairs for a minute. Please. Let me talk to Oscar. I'll be right up." She went. He turned back to Oscar, and talked softly.

"Haven't you ever heard of attorney-client privilege? I don't want her to know about this right now. I think you had better go. I have to calm her down."

"You want to plead to protect her. I understand that. But while you want to protect her, I want to protect you."

"I told you I don't want to talk about it anymore, and I don't. You're my lawyer, and I expect you to represent me in the way I ask."

"You know better than that, Roy. I have an ethical obligation to disclose any information that would show you didn't do it or that someone else did."

"Okay. You do what you have to do. Our stories will stand up. The fact is that we were together here most of the night. But not all night. She went out for a while, early in the evening. She seemed real excited when she came back. She might have killed him. I don't know for sure but I think so. To get him out of the way so we could be together. But I'm not going to let her go to jail.

"I really do love her, Oscar. It's something you maybe don't get." Roy said. His eyes were glassy.

Oscar hoped Roy wouldn't cry again.

He left the two of them and drove back to the gallery. Before leaving he arranged to meet with Lucy separately later that afternoon at her condo.

When he called Sheila she wasn't all that interested in the news.

"So they say they were together. So what? She's lying for her lover who just happens to be the killer of her husband. They probably worked together on it, planning to share the money and live happily ever after. It only strengthens my case against him, and almost makes a case against her. I could have conspiracy to add to the charges. You better have a serious talk with your boy, Leopold. The noose is tightening."

He hung up on her.

The situation was getting bizarre. What was this Rico asshole doing here and how were Lucy and Roy involved in it? Rico seemed to be convinced they were holding onto something valuable—something so important that Rico was risking arrest, jail, or worse to get it. His vague description of financial data didn't jibe with the approach he took and the threats. Roy or Lucy or both must know more than they revealed. And the law firm was a familiar one. Hard to believe Rico would drop the firm name and then threaten the three of them. As if he was their agent. Lawyers don't work that way. They already had the huge advantage of the legal process working for them. Maybe it was something else altogether and the firm wasn't involved at all. Maybe Rico was a loose cannon trying to clean up the mess from a job gone wrong.

Chapter Twenty-two

The Thursday morning *Palm Beach Post* had a surprise on the bottom of page one. Oscar spilled his coffee across his desk when he saw the article.

Timothy Bascomb had committed suicide.

NOTED ATTORNEY FOUND DEAD

APALACHICOLA, FL: One of the city's most respected attorneys was found dead early Monday morning. Timothy Bascomb, son of the late Apalachicola Mayor Malcolm Bascomb, was discovered at his office, the victim of an apparent suicide. He was reportedly not suffering from depression and the reason for his action is at this time unknown.

The senior partner of Bascomb, Hughes, & Riner, Timothy Bascomb took over the firm after his father's retirement and was largely responsible for its remarkable growth. His survivors include his wife of ten years, Catherine, and two children, Lisa and Matthew.

He read the article to Sydney, who had just wandered in from her room.

"There's something wrong with this picture. Why would Bascomb kill himself? And look at the date. They found him while we were over there. I had talked to him the day before."

"Coincidence. People kill themselves all the time. Especially lawyers, dentists and psychiatrists. High-pressure jobs. Maybe his wife was fooling around on him. Or just maybe he was afraid you were going to expose him. If he was in with that Walters guy then he would know that you have the goods on him." She sat in the chair opposite him while he dabbed up the spill.

"Could be, I suppose. He was a society bigwig over there. Maybe the idea of public disgrace, disbarment, and prison was too much for him to face. I hate to think I was the cause of it. On the other hand I didn't think they thought the situation was so far out of their control. These kinds of things can be tempered a lot. When you have the kind of power and money he had, a lot of things can be smoothed over. It just seems like an extreme response. I just wonder if it really was suicide or if he was in the way."

"In the way of who?"

"Maybe Walters and his boys. Could be that Walters is trying to clean up the possible witness list if things fall apart."

"What are you going to do?"

"I have to find this information he's after—if it exists, and take it to the police. At the very least I can show that Roy wasn't involved in Jack's scheme if that's what was going on. If it goes as far as trial I can use the information to cast some doubt on his guilt. I don't know. Sometimes I feel like I'm raking leaves in the wind."

He went into the gallery after first refilling his coffee and changing into dry pants. The street was quiet, as it usually was on Sunday mornings. There were only a few residences in the mostly commercial block. The buildings across the street were one story, a block-long row sharing an unbroken storefront. The gift shop and jewelry store would be open at noon. The insurance office and print shop were closed Sundays. An old man walking a dachshund puppy was coming toward him on his side of the street. The man was wearing a winter parka even though the morning temperature was in the low seventies. The dog was wearing a knit sweater of the same red color as the old man's coat. Jesse somehow sensed the other dog and began his obligatory barking downstairs.

Seeing the notice of Bascomb's death left him with mixed feelings. He was no friend to Oscar and they had met only that one day, but Oscar still felt somehow responsible for the death. What if he did it because of the information Oscar had questioned him about? Or maybe Bascomb was ready to crack anyway and this was just a good excuse. Attorneys were under a lot of pressure most of the time. He could testify to that, having had his own bout with depression and what his psychiatrist called an "episode requiring treatment." He went back upstairs. Murder seemed like a simpler explanation. He really needed to talk to Lucy.

Chapter Twenty-three

Lucy had always wanted to live in Palm Beach. The real Palm Beach on the barrier island, not the City of West Palm Beach on the mainland. And in the expensive area where people like the Kennedys and Trumps had their homes, not just one of the little apartments or condos crammed together near downtown. Jack hadn't been able to arrange it financially, even with the downturn in the housing market, though they did manage to get asked to a party or two. Big Jack told her they were invited just for comic relief, kind of like jesters. Lucy hoped they would make some friends with the insiders, and gradually work their way into the social scene. Maybe even be invited to join the country club. Never happened.

The residents of West Palm Beach and those of Palm Beach have always had an ongoing cultural battle, the rich versus the poor. There is disdain on both sides. The Palm Beach City Council even tried unsuccessfully to restrict access to the island city to residents only. But the social restrictions were more deep-seated than just being based on money. Even if Jack and Lucy had the net worth to live in one of the multimillion dollar homes, they doubtless wouldn't have been welcomed. Palm Beach society seemed to discriminate between new money and old money. If you had to earn your wealth you're not in the same category as those who inherited it. The fact that a new resident was incredibly rich didn't guarantee admission into the exclusive clubs. So the wannabees often settled for the areas near the island on the Intracoastal, yet close enough to call themselves Palm Beachers when they visited their summer homes and friends in the north.

Oscar had never been inside the Coast Meadow condominiums where Lucy, and formerly Big Jack, lived. The places were out of his league, starting in the high six figures. They were a modern geometric design with lots of glass and sharp angles. All were white stone with gray tile roofing and black solar glass. There were at least forty of them, but the area was heavily landscaped, and the drives twisted and turned so that only two or three could be seen at any one time.

He was expected. The security guard checked his name off a clipboard, and opened the gates to admit him. He caught a glimpse of the water as he turned to find Lucy's unit, number seven-thirteen.

He parked the Toyota in front of the closed garage door, and followed the sidewalk to the front entrance. Little gray lizards, chameleons or ginkgos, he thought they were called, skittered off the sun-warmed concrete in front of him, hiding in the shrubbery along the path.

The door opened before he rang the bell. Lucy was in a blue one-piece workout suit this time, the kind made of spandex that outlined her legs and butt in a different color than the rest of the outfit, giving the appearance of a string type bathing suit. She was in pretty nice shape, and obviously wanted him to see it.

But Oscar had already seen enough of her, and just wanted information. He worried that this thought process might mean he was getting old but still hoped she wasn't going to try a seduction scene. He unconsciously sucked in his stomach.

"Oscar. Come in."

He stepped inside, and she led him into the living room overlooking the water. The wall was floor to ceiling glass with two sliding doors at the side that opened to a brick patio and a three tiered concrete fountain splashing quietly. Like many of the better homes, the place was artfully decorated with sculpture and modern paintings. He thought one of his sculptures would look nice on a pedestal near the window. Maybe another outdoor piece for the patio?

"I'm sorry about this afternoon. I hope we can put that behind us." She smiled as he sat down. Was there a joke there?

"Can I get you a drink? I have everything. Soda, mineral water. How about beer?"

"Beer would be good."

She brought it in a glass, sipping on some sort of green mixed drink as she came in and sat opposite him on one of the matching wicker love seats. She put his glass on the coaster on the little glass side table.

"Nice place. Did you do the decorating?"

"Yes. It seems like a continuing project. Now with Jack gone I'm undecided as to whether to keep it. The insurance replaced the boat, so I have that to deal with. And I still haven't done anything with his clothes and things. You don't happen to know anyone who wears a size fifty-four by any chance?"

He shrugged and took another sip of the beer. "I'm a forty-two regular myself."

The small talk over, Lucy leaned forward, and her expression changed, the smiles all gone.

"I still think we should call the police about that guy. I mean, it sounded like he means to come back. I'm afraid."

"I'll call this Walters guy, maybe short circuit his thug. I expect he might have been behind the parking lot incident, and I've had enough of all that. This isn't at all like lawyers operate. Maybe Walters isn't involved at all. But if he is, what's he after? Are you sure there isn't something in Jack's records, something maybe incriminating Walters?"

"Like I said, I don't know of anything. But I'll keep looking. It might be in some of the stuff the cops took. I don't know." She shook her head slowly, looking at the floor as if contemplating the question then continued. "So how's the investigation going?" She sat with one leg crossed under her. Her drink was already almost gone, and she was lighting a cigarette. Oscar followed suit.

"Good. I found out a few things in Apalachicola that I thought you could explain for me."

She didn't flinch, but waited for him to continue.

"Tell me about the death of your first husband."

"My first husband is still alive."

Oscar's brain woke up a little more. "What?"

"I think he lives in Baton Rouge now, but I think you mean my second husband. The one who died in Apalachicola."

"That must be the one."

"Bobby. He was a sweetheart. I was really broken up about losing him."

"I don't mean to be callous, but didn't you marry Jack just after he died?"

"It wasn't just after. It was months. And Jack was very good to me after Bobby's death. I don't know how I could have handled it without him. We saw a lot of each other because of the lawsuit, and we just fell in love."

"You got quite a bit of money from that case didn't you?"

"I don't know that that's any of your business or that it has anything to do with the current situation. And no amount of money replaces a husband." She stood and walked to the window. She had forgotten about her cigarette until ashes spilled to the carpet. She opened the sliding glass door and tossed the butt outside.

"Sorry. I didn't mean to upset you. Let me change directions and start over. I'm trying to find out who else would have a motive to kill your husband."

"What does Apalachicola have to do with anything?" She turned toward me. "That was years ago. Maybe it was Walters," she said.

"Well, it did occur to me that Jack's death might have been business-related. I believe he may have had some sort of deal, just as you indicated, with various law firms around the state that may have started with a firm in Apalachicola. You were Jack's office manager. Was there any relationship with Bascomb, Hughes, & Riner that you know of? Anything more than just the normal litigation relationship?"

"No. We deal with firms all over Florida and the southeast part of the country. Some more than others, of course, because they work for particular insurance companies. But I don't know of any special arrangements or whatever you might want to call them. Regardless of what the papers say, lawyers don't kill other lawyers. They just sue each other. Money is their weapon."

"Why did the two of you move from Apalachicola after you married? Jack was already practicing law over there. Why not stay?"

"Big Jack had big ideas." She returned to sit opposite him again. "He wanted to come over to the East Coast where the action was. And he was right. He could never have built the size of business over there that he built here. This is nearer the population centers. The television stations, all the jobs, the people, and the money are right here."

"And you financed it all?"

"We were married. I had some money so we invested it in the business. And I think we're going beyond your area of investigation. Again."

The telephone rang. It was a land-line with one of those electronic buzzing rings that sound so untelephone-like. Lucy walked to the corner of the room and answered it, turning away from Oscar, and talking softly so that he wouldn't hear, but he could tell by the tone of her voice that she was angry with someone on the other end. She set the receiver down, and came back over to where he sat, and stood with her hands on her very nice hips. He wondered if she would consider modeling for him some time, but decided not to ask just yet.

"If that's all, Oscar?"

"One more thing, then I'll go."

She nodded, and then sat down, looking around for something distractedly, he assumed for her cigarettes.

"I understand you're going to get two and a half million dollars in life insurance proceeds."

"So what? And how did you know that anyway? Jack took care of me like he should have. He did nothing different than any big executive running a big business would do. Besides, there are debts I have to take care of."

"It's a lot of money. Did the police know about the circumstances of your first, make that second, husband's death?"

"What do you mean?" She lit another cigarette, and tossed the pack on the glass-topped table, then clicked the lighter off and on nervously.

"Did they ask you about losing two husbands in boat explosions and collecting fortunes on both of them?"

"What are you trying to get at?" She blew smoke into his face.

"It just seems curious, almost too coincidental, and both times you have another guy waiting in the wings ready to soothe your broken heart."

She stood.

"Look, you son of a bitch." Her eyes flashed, "You get out of my house right now. Roy is going to hear about this. I don't know if you're making some feeble attempt at extortion or are accusing me of murder. Either way I want you the fuck out of here. If you want to go to the police then go. I have nothing to hide. Now get out!"

"Another thing before I go. What do you know about the death of Timothy Bascomb?"

"Nothing. Now leave."

He left, wondering why he couldn't get an easy confession like the investigators did on television.

Lucy was shaking with rage after Leopold left. She found her empty glass, took it to the bar, and filled it with vodka, adding only two ice cubes. She had never liked him, even though he was a close friend of Roy's. The jerk had no ambition. He dressed badly and didn't respect his own profession. He was a fucking lawyer but wouldn't act like one. She gulped down half the drink, and set the glass down too hard on the bar top, then began to cry softly.

She looked up, hearing a light tap on the patio door. She had been expecting him and was relieved to see him again. He entered the room from the patio, and they embraced tenderly but tightly. Lucy broke free after a moment.

"Do you think he knows anything? Anything for sure?" she asked.

"I'll find out. Don't worry. It's almost over."

Chapter Twenty-four

Sydney returned late that night, pleasantly surprising Oscar who had planned a default evening of watching reruns of CSI. For now he sat on the second story balcony overlooking the street. Streetlights situated near the building meant that neither the balcony nor his bedroom window were ever in complete darkness so Oscar had never tried to turn on the outdoor floodlights that were mounted high up on the front of the building.

The streetlights annoyed him so much when he first bought the place that he had shot them out with an air pistol late one night, thinking he would be unnoticed. The crashing glass had made quite a noise, however. The police came, he didn't answer the door, and the lights were replaced within the week. Now he just lived with them. When Sydney learned of the problem she got a ladder, sprayed black paint on the sides of the lights facing his building and eliminated the problem. A simple solution.

He was watching the day end and imagined that he could barely make out the ocean off in the distance between two tree-tops, though he knew it was behind him, and nearly three miles away. The sun had already set, and only an occasional mosquito visited this high off the ground.

Sydney let herself in and joined him. They sat back in the two aging Adirondack chairs and rested their feet on the wrought iron railing. She was fetchingly dressed in an iridescent blue top and matching mini-shorts. He admired the little freckles on her tanned chest before he spoke.

"Want a drink?" he asked.

"Yup. Hard day at work, huh? Me, too." She reached down beside her, and pulled out an already opened bottle of Pinot Grigio from a paper bag she had brought in with her. No glasses. She took a slug and passed it to him. It was chilled.

"That's right. I forgot that you're a full time legal secretary now. Have you found out anything good yet?"

"Some spymaster you'd make, losing track of your agents."

"So?"

"I do have the address and phone number of this Billy Grubbs guy who was causing trouble at the office, remember? He was one of the clients Jack apparently screwed out of their money."

"Good. I'll go see him."

"It won't be that easy. He seems to have skipped town. I tried calling him, and his girlfriend says he's been gone for a couple of weeks. Her exact words were, 'The big fat son of a bitch is off fucking some whore, and I don't give a shit if he never comes back.'" Sydney imitated the heavy Southern accent. "But she said it wasn't all that unusual, and she expected that he would show up sometime."

"Did you get into the computer?" Oscar took another tipple of wine.

"No problem with the general office system. It's networked, and everybody can get in with the same password. But there are two separate systems, the other probably for the financials. I can't get into that one. It takes a different password."

"Doesn't anyone know what it is?"

She punched him lightly on the shoulder. "I tried. The other girl I'm working with said it was Jack's, and had nothing to do with the case activity. I'm supposed to be an undercover agent. I can't very well tell them I want to search through his private records, can I?"

"Why not? All they can do is tell you no. My mother always said that if you haven't been told no at least three times every day, you haven't asked for enough."

"Do you do that?"

"Not me. But it's an interesting way of looking at life, kind of an assertive life attitude.

"Is it possible, Sydney, to copy the computer records without actually getting into them with the password?" He knew next to nothing about computers except how to turn on and operate his word processing program, send email, and do some Googling.

"No. What I need is the password or enough time sitting in front of it to hack into it."

"We need to visit the office when there aren't so many people around," Oscar said.

"A break-in? Aren't you in enough trouble already?"

"Let's just call it private in-depth investigation. And you work there. I would be coming as your guest. Are you free tomorrow night?"

"Sounds like a date to me."

They had to wait until evening to get access to the firm's computer. Sydney went on into work. Even though it was Saturday, the office was open for employees, since many of the associates worked weekends to control the current disarray of the client files. Oscar spent the day wrapping up the other two legal clients he had, two estate-planning clients moving here fresh from New York State, and prepared a discovery motion on Roy's case to file with the court on Monday. He continued to duck reporters and considered having the words *no comment, but my client is innocent* printed on a lapel badge.

The artist from Chicago called, and Oscar confirmed the opening of her show and told her everything had arrived undamaged. He called the printer and had a proof of the announcement e-mailed directly to Chicago. Sydney met Oscar for lunch at Mary Lou's Country Kitchen, near the gallery, and Oscar discussed the computer situation.

There was no longer a Mary Lou at Mary Lou's. The owner was a Nicaraguan exile who thought keeping the name would bring in the Anglos. Once inside, the customers were served black beans and rice and a pitcher of hot milk with every order. Oscar likened it to the practice of a restaurant he had once frequented in Alabama that automatically gave every customer a cup of coffee and a bowl of grits to start when they came in for breakfast.

Oscar had eaten at Mary Lou's even before he bought the gallery building. It changed hands every two years or so. The menu was usually different, but the place always looked the same. The wallpaper was imprinted with pelicans and flamingos, but they got a little more stained and greasy each year. The plastic flowers in the wall sconces never wilted, and the tables and chairs were sturdy chrome steel and red Formica that would last forever. The blades of the slow-moving ceiling fan were encrusted with a greasy black coating. Oscar always made sure he didn't pick a table near the fan since he sometimes saw pieces of the grime fly off the ends of the blades.

Oscar ordered the unnamed daily special, trusting that it would be edible, and Sydney ordered something in Spanish.

"You ordered the special—don't you want to know what it is?"

"I like to be surprised."

"You don't know any Spanish? This is South Florida. Being bilingual would be an asset."

"In fact, I'm multilingual. I can order beer in four languages. I figure I know the essentials of international communication."

Sydney began explaining various ways to hack into the office computer. Oscar, ignorant of the terminology, stopped her. She always had the skills he needed, but would never explain satisfactorily how she had acquired them. Oscar speculated, half seriously, that Sydney was a part-time government secret agent or maybe on the run from a former life, perhaps in the witness protection program. Or maybe he was overwhelmed by her Renaissance woman skills because of his own limited areas of expertise. Her skills seemed to be a shotgun, while he was more of a rifle.

Sydney was served a cheeseburger and fries. Oscar got a plate of tortillas, refried beans and rice, all covered with melted cheese and sprinkled with shredded iceberg lettuce and chopped tomatoes and onions. The cheeseburger looked better.

After lunch, Sydney went back to work, and Oscar finished hanging the paintings for the show.

The Buick engine made a harsh rattling noise when he started it, and Oscar listened closely, trying to diagnose the problem. He finally decided it had a bad noise, shut it off, and called Angelo to come get it. The Toyota worked. He took the twenty-five-caliber automatic out of the Buick and put it in the Toyota, which unfortunately didn't have a working lock on the glove compartment. The car's tires were so bald the metal threads from the steel belted radials were showing through the shiny smooth spots. He thought it would be okay for around town. Just stay off the freeways and drive slowly.

Sydney was dressed all in black when she got in the car, like a ninja warrior from Saturday morning cartoons, and was ready to smear black makeup on her face when Oscar stopped her.

"No need for that. If we get caught, we don't want to look too suspicious."

"If we get caught, it won't matter." She put the makeup away.

He backed out, the squashing tangerines making soft sounds, turned on the headlights, and pulled down the alley into the street.

Sydney had the key so breaking in was no problem. She first disarmed the security system. He watched her punch in the code: 2,4,6,8. Not a very clever number but maybe so obvious that no one would guess it. She left the lights off and led him into the main office work area. The large room was divided into cubicles with portable fabric covered shoulder-high dividers.

Every cubicle they passed was equipped with a computer terminal, an L-shaped desk, and a chair. Most had memos tacked to the dividers and personal stuff like pictures and small potted plants sitting around. In the computer room she closed the door and turned on the lights. It had no outside windows.

"This is it." She pointed to the lone computer set up on one side of the room.

"You mean that's all there is to it?" Oscar asked. He had envisioned a huge mainframe with spinning disks, lots of dials, and flashing lights. What she pointed to were two standard-sized monitors, one keyboard, and two white rectangular boxes sitting on end under the table with little slots and doors in the front. There were other boxes and cables but the whole thing wasn't that big.

"That's the whole computer?"

Sydney sat in front of the monitor and turned it on. "The system doesn't take up much space like it used to. Just the CPU, monitors, and printer. Each desk has its own monitor networked into this main unit. In fact this is old technology; it could be a lot simpler. Let me get to work."

Oscar left her alone since there was nothing for him to do until they got the information out of it. He decided to keep watch, wandering through the office, looking in doorways.

Then he saw Jack's office.

He knew it was Jack's because of the nameplate on the door. Good detective work. He had never been in this office, but it was just as cluttered as the one he had visited in Jack's old office building several years ago. As if they had moved the whole mess intact. Inside, it was big. Not as big as Tim Bascomb's, but big. The carpeting must have had several layers of padding underneath because it felt spongy, almost bouncy, like walking on a tight trampoline. Stacks of file folders, newspapers, and magazines were everywhere. The oversized desk was rosewood or some other exotic material, and the desk chair was like a huge brown leather La-Z-Boy recliner on wheels. Jack had been a big guy and needed big stuff, Oscar guessed.

He used his shirt-sleeve to open the drawers, thinking he was probably being silly, but didn't want to leave prints. Just the usual desk things inside. He leafed through some of the files on the desk, but there were hundreds scattered about and he didn't really know where to begin. Most of them looked like pending client files and probably would offer no useful information.

On impulse he pulled the center drawer all the way out and looked under it. He had once seen a television show where the secret documents were taped to the bottom of a drawer. Nothing there. No hidden wall safes behind the pictures either.

He checked the parking lot again through the window and was heading back to the computer room when a light flashed through the office from outside. A police spotlight maybe? He froze. The light passed through again, briefly illuminating the office cubicles in turn. He crept up to the window facing the front of the building and peeked out. A car was out front backing into a parking space, someone unexpectedly coming in to work to finish a brief or pick up a file?.

He rushed back to the computer room.

"Wrap it up fast! Someone is coming in any second! Did you get the information?"

"No time to break in," Sydney said. "I need another half hour, maybe more."

"Take the whole thing," Oscar said.

"What do you mean, take the whole thing?" They stood at the door of the computer room and Sydney had just flipped off the light switch.

"The computer. We can each take a piece and get the hell out. We'll finish it later.

Oscar checked the window again. The car still had its lights on, so they had a minute at least.

"Take whatever you need. Wipe off your fingerprints from everything. Maybe take the keyboard, too. Where do they keep the petty cash?"

Sydney was hurriedly disconnecting one of the units on the floor. "It's in the receptionist's desk. Why?"

"We have to make it look like a burglary. I'll get the petty cash and dump a few drawers. Let's get out of here."

They hit the rear door about thirty seconds later. Sydney had handed Oscar one piece of the computer, the larger CPU. She re-armed the burglar alarm, locked the door, and ran to the car. Oscar stopped, picked up a small landscaping brick and broke out the window next to the back door. No alarm went off. He jumped in the car, and they crept out of the lot with their lights off.

"Silent alarm?" Sydney asked.

"I hope so. I never set one off before. Do you think the police will buy the burglary idea?"

"I doubt it. You can't just reach in through the window and unlock the door. You need a key from either side"

Sydney jumped out of the car, ran to the back door and did one of those spin-in-the-air-and-kick karate moves. The wooden door frame splintered and the door slammed open. She ran back and jumped behind the wheel.

"*Now* they'll think it looks like a burglary." She pulled into traffic, headlights on, working through the lanes circling the block, they passed the front of the office and the car that had been there was gone. False alarm.

"I'll be in tomorrow morning. Maybe we can return the computer before then if I can get into it sooner."

Chapter Twenty-five

They passed a police car going the opposite direction with its emergency lights on and siren off and both started laughing.

Sydney let them into her room. Oscar hadn't been in there since she had moved downstairs.

"Now don't ask any questions about things you might see in here, and don't touch anything." She looked directly at Oscar, "I don't want you getting hurt from things you don't know how to handle. No offense."

The room was brightly lit. Sydney had installed fluorescents in place of the single ceiling fixture that had been there before. It was a sizeable windowless room with high, old-fashioned, coved tin ceilings. A white three-bladed ceiling fan, also her addition, spun slowly. One wall was shelving and tables with cabinets underneath. To the left was an elaborate computer setup. To Oscar's uneducated eye hers looked more imposing than the one in Jack's law office. Mostly because she had more components. There were three computer monitors. The single bed in the corner was almost an afterthought. A worktable covered with books was in the center of the room. The small kitchen area and bath were to the right of the door.

He saw the mounted assault rifle and started toward it.

"Don't," Sydney said. "It's full auto and loaded. I don't want you to get hurt—or worse, shoot me by accident."

"What do you need with that?" Oscar wondered about the kind of interests she had when she wasn't working as an investigator and computer hacker.

"Just a hobby. Let's say I'm a gun enthusiast. Now take a look at this data." She spent several minutes connecting her equipment to the stolen CPU, started it, and began punching the keyboard. In only a few minutes of entering commands she said, "Voila!" and pushed back to display the screen for them.

Oscar looked over her shoulder at several columns of numbers and letters. About three-quarters of them had what looked like plaintiff and defendant names as well.

"How did you get the password?" Oscar asked.

Sydney went back to the keyboard. "Most people use names, birthdays, house numbers, stuff like that. Then you have to fool around with upper and lower case since a lot of them are case sensitive. Trial and error is the quickest way if it works and I have a program on my computer that runs all the various combinations. This time it did. Bigjack1957. His nickname and year of birth.

"Do you recognize anything from this list?" Sydney asked.

"Can you print it out? How long is it?" Oscar did better with hard copy. Sydney pressed another key or two and the laser printer began spitting out sheet after sheet of data. Oscar picked up the first one.

"I think I recognize something. Some of these look like case numbers for court files. Others could be attorney code numbers. We all have one assigned by the state bar, and next to that is what must be a date, then a number that I don't know the meaning of."

Sydney was looking at the screen, not the paper.

"Could be other ID numbers, client numbers, or maybe dollar amounts."

"That must be it," Oscar said. "I can take some of these numbers down to the courthouse and look up the attorney numbers to see who we're dealing with. Or maybe get them from my bar directory. It will take time but I might be able to see the significance of the numbers here. It might just be the record of cases and settlements. Nothing exotic. But you never know."

"No need to go to all that trouble," Sydney said. "We're in the information age. Take a ride on the info highway."

She began pressing keys again. Oscar gave up trying to figure out what she was doing and stood back with his hands in his pockets waiting. He imagined this must be what it felt like to be a woman, waiting and watching while a man changed your tire. You could just as easily wander off and come back when the job was done, but somehow felt an obligation to watch the other person work, as if being there was actually helping. He didn't take his eyes off the screen.

"How about a cup of coffee or a drink?"

"Not now. I have it, I think. There." Sydney slid back from the screen so they could both see. "Now we have a list of all the attorney ID numbers from the State Bar computer in Tallahassee and if this works out," she began playing the computer keyboard like she was playing a piano, "We can, yes, we can get a list of all pending cases in the whole state system from the state court administrator's office. Now when we cross reference these with the list we started out with"—she kept punching—"we get a new list with names of attorneys and case names, arranged any way you like, by attorney or date or alphabetically by client, you name it. That takes care of the ones with court file numbers. It's a simple Excel program. Not all of them have court file numbers, so I assume these were settled prior to filing."

Oscar clapped her on the shoulder. "Give me separate lists of the attorneys for each defendant in cases handled by Jack's firm."

He got them. By the time they were through, they had a list which looked to be entirely cases handled personally by Roy Flagler, not Big Jack. Dollar amounts were divided into two columns, the net plaintiff attorney fee per case and a second amount that looked to be twenty-five percent of that next to the defense attorney's name for that case. Payoffs?

They all involved only fifteen defense attorneys, and over fifty-percent were divided among only three defense lawyers:

Timothy Bascomb, Carl Seacliff of Miami, and Robert Jerome Walters of Fort Lauderdale. The senior partners of three of the biggest insurance defense firms in the state. Maybe it made sense and nothing was amiss. But it looked bad. It looked like kickbacks and collusion to Oscar. While referral fees to other attorneys was common and accepted, sharing money with the opposing counsel was a big no-no. The dollar amounts were astronomical. He had Sydney run a total, and it was in excess of twelve million dollars. That averaged out to two million a year. Where did all that money go? Roy didn't live like he had gotten it.

It was time to talk to Roy and Lucy again.

"This can't be right," Oscar said.

"Why not? It's Jack's personal files," Sydney said. "Looks to me like Jack and Roy were in on this together. I know you're defending him, Oscar, but it looks like Roy had good motivation here. Get rid of Big Jack and keep the money for himself. He probably has it squirreled away somewhere waiting for you to get him off the hook. The information here will hang him."

"I hope you're wrong," Oscar said. "Roy wouldn't do anything like this. I know him better than anybody."

"Money, a lot of money that is, does strange things to people. And maybe you don't know as much about him as you think."

Sydney put the compiled data on a finger-sized flash drive for Oscar. She erased any evidence of her entry into the files from the computer, changed the password to make it very difficult to crack, unhooked the hardware, and said she would get to the office early and maybe drop it into the shrubbery near the parking lot to be discovered later. They didn't want to stand accused of conspiring to destroy evidence. The police would think it was dropped by the burglars on the way out. Oscar took one printout and the flash drive, put them in a manila envelope and went to the office safe. It came with the building and he rarely used it. It was a huge Mosler, about five feet high. It was on rollers but was so heavy he couldn't move it, so it stayed in the corner. It was almost a work of art, about five feet tall, black with gold lettering, *Mosler Safe & Lock Company* in script. There was even a picture painted on the door. A landscape. It had cost him three hundred dollars to get a safe company to open it and change the combination. He put the envelope inside. Only his old tax returns shared the space.

The problem now was Roy. Had he been stealing from the firm, maybe in collusion with Lucy? Was he indeed up to his neck in this fraudulent deal with Big Jack? Did he kill him after all? Sometimes we believe what we want to believe against all evidence to the contrary.

Chapter Twenty-six

CNN Headline News was featuring the Big Jack Gamble case all day Sunday. Oscar watched as the commentator stood in front of the courthouse discussing the Lawyer Killing Lawyer Case, and explained how the attorney for the defendant refused to be interviewed. There was a short segment with Sheila complaining about the judge allowing Roy out on bail. They cut away to shots of the burned-out hulk of Jack's boat, then followed up with an "interesting side story" of Oscar's own pending criminal charges. They interviewed Carlos Sanchez in the hospital, where he told a one-sided story of an attorney gone amok, shooting down defenseless kids in a parking lot.

Oscar shut the television off, trying to decide if he should give some interviews. Maybe some big-time Hollywood producer would want to buy the rights to his story. It could be a television miniseries or at least a made-for-cable thriller.

Usually Oscar skipped breakfast, drinking five or six cups of coffee before lunch instead. Sydney had stopped in to make him a "magnificent feast of a meal," so Oscar worked on his long delayed laundry while Sydney did the kitchen thing in her usual athletic shorts, T-shirt, and sandals, but adding an apron imprinted in red letters with *Nobody Knows I'm A Lesbian* and a white ball cap she wore backwards.

Oscar's kitchen wasn't exactly state-of-the-art, but he did have two good cast-iron skillets and an assortment of hand-made porcelain bowls given to him in exchange for one of his small sculptures by Kelly, a not quite skinny, but almost pretty nineteen-year-old potter who had once rented part of the studio. She decided to move her studio to her parents' basement when Oscar wouldn't take any more pottery for rent.

The stove was an ancient gas two-burner. The oven worked only on high, but the flames were good for char grilling a steak real fast if he kept the windows open to prevent the smoke alarm from going off. Oscar did most of his cooking in the coffee pot and microwave. Having a reputation as a non-cooker meant that people, men and women, felt compelled to cook for him. He had little incentive to learn.

There was no dishwasher, but he owned few dishes, so the lack had never been a problem. His stackable combination clothes washer-dryer unit was in the corner of the kitchen behind a set of louvered sliding doors that were always falling off the track.

"Oscar. You're a lawyer. Aren't you embarrassed to live like this?" Sydney was frying something with eggs, cheese, onions, potatoes and garlic in both pans

"Like what?"

"Like a destitute college kid. You could be in a nice house or condo near the beach for God's sake."

"Did that. This is better."

Oscar was transferring his socks and underwear from the washer to the dryer when his cell phone rang.

That meant it was either a salesperson auto dialing numbers in sequence, or someone he knew well. He had two lines, upstairs and down, for the law office and the gallery. Only nine people that he knew of had the cell number. No name, just a number on the caller ID.

"Hey," Oscar said, expecting to hear a familiar voice.

"Mr. Leopold, listen carefully."

"Who is this?"

"I said listen carefully, and you will understand. You don't know me. My name is R.J. Walters."

"Robert Jerome Walters? With the psycho son Rico?"

"Why, yes. So you do know of me. And Rico," he hesitated, "I must meet with you. Now would be a good time. Is that a problem?"

"Actually," he signalled to Sydney to turn off the stove. She had heard Oscar say the name and recognized it, too. "Actually, I am just sitting down to breakfast. Maybe later this afternoon you could drive up to see me."

"Look outside, Mr. Leopold. In front of your building."

He walked to the front window to look down to the street. A white Mercedes stretch limo with six doors and blacked out windows sat in the loading zone. He returned to the telephone.

"So?"

"So the car is here for your convenience. A nice ride to my office. Just go on down, get in, and in an hour we can discuss the Jack Gamble situation."

"I am just sitting down to eat with a close friend, Mr. Walters. Besides, I have a car. I can be there maybe tomorrow, maybe not. In fact, I have an office here. Why don't you come on up to see me."

"I am afraid I must insist. There are two men in the car who will assist you if you won't come willingly. Please make it easy on yourself, and you won't be sorry. I promise."

He hung up.

Oscar told Sydney what Walters said.

"So you want to call the cops or take these guys on ourselves? I'm equipped to handle it, believe me." Sydney took her apron off. Rico again, and here. She wasn't surprised since she now knew of his relationship with the recently deceased attorney Bascomb. She didn't think he knew she was here. But he did know her face.

"I believe you, believe me, but no. I think I should go see what he wants. He's not likely to do anything to me, since you know where I'm going."

"Okay, but take me with you." By going she would give up her location and probably have to relocate, but Oscar would be safer. Choices have to be made sometimes.

"You're what, a hundred pounds dripping wet? No. You follow and be ready to call the police if anything goes wrong."

"Okay, but to be safe, let's use a wire. Otherwise how will I know when to make the call?" Sydney headed downstairs to her room. Oscar followed.

"A wire? You mean some kind of hidden microphone?"

Sydney rummaged through a drawer and pulled out a small round black button with a thin wire protruding from the side. She made an adjustment to it and handed it to Oscar.

"Just drop this in your shirt pocket. I'll follow you with the receiver. I can pick up anything anyone says within about twenty-five feet of this, so long as I am no more than a couple hundred yards away from it. I can record it, and if they admit anything, we'll have them on tape. If you get into trouble, I can come in like gangbusters and help out."

Sounded like a better plan to Oscar than anything he had going, so he dropped it into his shirt pocket and headed toward the front door.

"Sydney, much as I hate to say this, take the Mustang. I don't want any car trouble fouling this up."

To be extra safe Sydney grabbed a vintage Colt .45 Army pistol along with an extra clip and dropped them into her bag.

Oscar decided that if Walters wanted him dead, he would have done it by now and not sent a car for him. Rico, the guy who had accosted him in Roy's house, held the back door of the limo open for Oscar when he came outside. The guy looked like the ones who stood around the casino on Paradise Island in Nassau, wearing expensive suits, just watching everything. He introduced himself, as if they hadn't met previously, closed the door, and joined his companion in the front. With the privacy screen up neither could talk to Oscar. He checked out the liquor supply in the little portable bar, but decided to keep a clear head. A few minutes later, he was getting nervous and changed his mind. It might be his last drink. He had a double cognac.

The driver took US-1 all the way to Fort Lauderdale. Oscar suggested I-95 or even the turnpike, but the driver ignored him. Maybe he couldn't hear through the glass. The road was heavily congested day and night. From West Palm all the way south seventy miles to Miami, the roadway was flanked by hundreds of nearly identically styled strip malls, high rises, and storefronts, all of them of pastel-colored stucco in a bastardized Spanish architecture. It was impossible to tell, other than by the signs, the border lines between towns they passed through.

Seeing a vacant parcel of land was unusual. Even then it was generally under construction. The building boom in Florida had continued unabated since the late fifties and only slowed with the 2008 recession. Too many people, too many cars. Near Fort Lauderdale off the main drag were hundreds of older small motels, many with permanent residents. Huge condo towers obscured every available view of the ocean on the Southeast Florida coastline, save those few rare areas reserved for public beaches.

They pulled into a private parking garage under a multistory office building in Fort Lauderdale. All three got out, entered the elevator, Oscar first, and arrived at the seventeenth floor. The receptionist greeted Rico with "good morning, Mr. Walters," and went back to her work. Several young lawyer types were walking through the area, carrying files and talking quietly.

"Do you have the whole seventeenth floor?" he said to Rico on his left and to his pocket. He hoped Sydney was getting this. She would at least know where he was.

"Three floors."

Rico led him through double glass doors, down a hallway, and deposited him in a large private corner office with a view of the ocean through its many windows. The desk seemed almost an afterthought in the tastefully furnished room. Original paintings, contemporary sculpture, and a furniture grouping around an oriental rug looked like a picture from a decorating magazine. Behind the print sofa was a two-hundred-gallon saltwater fish tank. He walked over to see it more closely. The sole resident was a large toothy moray eel poking its head out from the rocks and coral.

"So good of you to come, Mr. Leopold."

He turned. Startled. He hadn't heard the door open.

"My name is R.J. Walters, as you must know, and I believe you have already met my son and assistant, Rico."

"I hope it's nice meeting you." Oscar didn't take Walters' extended hand. Walters exuded wealth. He had that carefully tanned, tailored, and manicured look that made him look fit and youthful even though he had to be at least seventy. His face had a tightness and sheen that suggested plastic surgery some years ago. As a sculptor Oscar knew the signs a body gives as it ages, and these had been altered on Mr. Walters. But not everything. The ears continue to grow as you age and are not easily tailored by any kind of surgery.

"Nice view of the beach from here," he said for Sydney.

"First things first. Give me your transmitter." Rico held out his hand.

Oscar must have looked surprised, ready to deny it when Rico continued. "We're quite sophisticated here, Mr. Leopold. Your transmitter was detected by our equipment as soon as you arrived on the floor."

Oscar scooped it out and handed it to him. "Mind if I sit down?"

"Not at all."

Rico handed it to R.J., who dropped the little microphone into the aquarium. The moray moved ever so slightly. Walters walked to the fish tank. He picked up a small hand net, scooped a freshwater goldfish out of a small glass bowl on the table nearby and dropped the fish into the aquarium. It swam crazily through the water and weeds, in obvious distress from the saltwater.

"You see, Mr. Leopold? Here we have an example analogous to you, and to Jack Gamble. The little fish is out of its element. It will struggle mightily and die ultimately, but sometimes an intervening force brings things to an end even more quickly."

The small darting fish disappeared in an instant when it shot to the bottom of the tank near a small coral cave and was snapped into the sharp-toothed mouth of the waiting moray eel.

"You can have your transmitter back when you leave if you want to retrieve it. Now if you would be so kind, please remove your clothing."

Oscar was incredulous. "My clothing?" Was this guy a pervert or was this his idea of foreplay?

"I am quite serious. Mr. Leopold. I want to be absolutely sure I have missed nothing. Technology today may mean you have some other sort of device on you and we don't take chances. That's why I wanted to talk to you here. I can be absolutely certain no one but the three of us will be a party to this conversation.

"If you prefer, I can have Rico here cut your clothes off with his knife. He's quite expert with it, I can tell you."

Rico removed a shiny stiletto from his boot as evidence and inducement. "I'm not fucking around here pal." Rico reached over, grabbed Oscar by the belt, and sliced it in two.

"Okay, Okay. Pervert." Oscar took off his clothing and shoes, folded them, and set them on the closest chair. Rico picked them up and took them into an adjacent room. Now he did feel foolish. Where to put his hands? What is nudist etiquette? Maybe the microphone had made Walters mad. What was Sydney going to do? Charge in like gangbusters as she said? She must have heard them ask for the transmitter.

"This is a little technique I learned from Rico and his training some time ago. I find people so much less belligerent and much more forthcoming with answers when they're unclothed. Perhaps it is a sense of vulnerability. Do you feel that way Mr. Leopold?"

Oscar knew Walters thought he was clever, and in truth Oscar did feel ridiculous and embarrassed. And angry. He tried to hold his stomach in and be casual, as if he often sat around naked in other people's offices having a business meeting.

"Would you like a drink?"

"No, thanks. Get this game of yours over with. Bullshit like this has a way of coming back to bite you in the ass."

"Easy now. I think we have some business to discuss."

"What business is that?"

"We're brother attorneys, Mr. Leopold, albeit on different levels of the legal world, but I can speak frankly. Especially now. You have something we're quite interested in, something that could prove to be a problem to my associates and myself if it were to fall into the wrong hands."

"And what might that be?" Oscar wished he had taken more than one drink.

"The computer records. We know you have a copy of them. We're aware of the break-in last night. Now, I've managed to get possession of the original computer and have destroyed the records inside, but I assume you made a copy." He sat across from Oscar on the other sofa and leaned back.

"I can make it worth your while, of course. I don't expect you to walk away from this empty-handed. You have something I need and I am willing to pay. Fifty thousand dollars. We'll call it a legal consulting fee to make it completely unquestionable. Or, if you prefer, I will give you cash. Your choice."

"And I get my clothes back, too?" Oscar had had enough and was thinking now of payback.

Walters smiled. "What do you say? Do we have an understanding?"

"I don't know what's so interesting about these computer records you're talking about." It was a little chilly in the office. The air conditioning duct was blowing right across Oscar's shoulders. He shivered.

"I looked at them, sure, but it was just a series of names and numbers. Didn't help me. I'm trying to find something that will clear my client. That's all. I have no interest in computer records. That's why I didn't make a copy. It didn't help, so I had everything put back."

Oscar thought they must have been planning their own break in of the office when he beat them to it. The car that arrived last night must have been Walters' people, and they had followed the getaway.

Walters stared at Oscar for a minute or two saying nothing. Oscar hoped he saw no percentage in killing him.

"You need to understand what's at stake here. I am responsible for the livelihoods of dozens of people who work for me. When I discovered that Rico had been making under-the-table deals with Gamble, I had to make a decision. Either cover it up or turn him in. I think you know that the fallout from that sort of thing would destroy this firm. I couldn't let that happen. I tried to put an end to it, but Gamble would have none of it. Now that he's gone I need all the evidence disappeared."

"I told you I don't have it. Are you the one who killed Big Jack?"

"All right, Mr. Leopold. You think things are so easy. We will be in touch again. Think over my offer carefully. I'll give you three days. Remember the goldfish. Rico will tell you how to contact me if you make the right decision before then. If you think you can hold me up for more money, you're quite mistaken. This offer expires soon." He stood. "And so may you."

Oscar was allowed to dress and leave with no interference. He dropped the two pieces of his severed belt in the fish tank.

He left the microphone there. When the elevator door opened Sydney leaped out, gun in hand, saw Oscar waiting, and jumped back in.

"Gangbusters," he said to her.

"Shut up."

As they pushed through the revolving entrance door on the ground floor, who was going the opposite way? Carl Cake, Roy's former client. Oscar continued circling in the revolving door until he was back inside, leaving Sydney on the sidewalk. Cake was walking toward the elevators and hadn't noticed him. Oscar waited. Cake got on alone. The elevator stopped at the seventeenth floor.

They walked out into the bright sunshine, Oscar holding his pants up with one hand, wishing he had his sunglasses. There was a pair in the Mustang. There was no limo in sight.

They walked to the municipal parking near the beach, only one block down. This was the weather that made living in Florida worthwhile, despite the crowds and crime. It was about seventy-five degrees with a light breeze, low humidity, and blue skies. Sydney dropped into the driver's seat, put the top down, and put on Oscar's sunglasses.

"I could have saved you."

"It went okay. But I lost the bug."

Oscar hopped into the passenger side and they pulled away, slowing to let three blonde college-age girls in tiny red bikinis cross to the beach.

"I love spring break," he mused wistfully.

He had dated one or two girls that age after his divorce, but considered them just that. Girls. They had nothing in common with him, and he had to admit he was primarily attracted to them physically. Not that that was all bad. Lately, though, what older guys had told him turned out to be true. Women that age gave him as much attention as they did a utility pole. One thing he had learned, to his regret, was that young women were primarily interested in young men. Or maybe nowadays in other young women.

"Put the top up," Oscar said. "The sun will ruin the upholstery. And get your own sunglasses."

Sydney pulled over to put the top up.

He explained what had happened on the way back to West Palm. He left out the part about having to strip, thinking it didn't contribute to the story.

Chapter Twenty-seven

The first person Oscar suspected of burglarizing his building was attorney Walters, who had just been telling Oscar he wanted the records. It seemed too much of a coincidence that while they were talking, someone was ransacking his place. The thing was, though, that R.J.'s go-to man for thug work was Rico, and he could not have done it.

Sydney went to her room immediately, but whoever it was hadn't been able to get through her steel door. The dents and footprints on it indicated they had tried. The rest of the place was a mess. The gallery was intact. The studio and office were tossed, along with the upstairs apartment, though Sydney said she didn't see much difference.

Oscar went to the safe, confident they wouldn't have been able to break into it.

They hadn't.

The safe was gone. He could see the marks on the floor where it had been skidded to the back door, then chipped concrete on the one step down to the parking area. Had to be several guys. Had to have a truck. Probably a hydraulic lift gate or a tow truck to lift the thing. He checked with Angelo down the alley, who said he hadn't seen anything. So somebody had the information implicating Roy, but it also revealed the payoffs and fraud.

Oscar hoped that now they would leave him alone, having gotten what they wanted. He wondered if he should call and ask for the fifty thousand he had been offered. Odds were they wouldn't turn in the documents, since they would be implicating themselves too. Would this end it? Roy was still on the hook for the murder.

Maybe Roy knew about the computer records. The data was damning and Oscar needed to know whether the information was correct. It would have helped if he had had the records themselves, but he remembered the gist of them. Maybe Roy could help him with the rest. And what about the statement Walters made about having the computer?

First thing the next morning, he called Sydney at Big Jack's office to see how they had reacted to the burglary. After waiting for the computerized telephone answering system to give him all his options, he was finally able to talk to a live person who put him through to her.

"Oscar! There was a break-in here over the weekend."

"Are you saying that for the people around you or do you mean a break-in besides the one we pulled off?"

"Both. Someone came in and stole the computer system. The office is in a real mess now. Even the back-up tapes are gone."

"Did you plant the computer box in the bushes earlier this weekend?"

"Yes. But it's gone. Also all the office financial records, billings, everything the police didn't take earlier is gone. It'll take months to recreate the records from the files themselves."

"Don't worry. You won't be working there that long. Not your problem. Come on back here as soon as you can. Make an excuse. We don't need you there any more. Is Lucy working today?"

"Yes. Why do you ask?"

"Just wondered. See you later."

Oscar almost decided to call the police to report the burglary at his place then changed his mind. He knew who had done it, but couldn't prove anything. Nothing other than the safe and the computer records were damaged or missing, so there was no reason for a police report or an insurance claim. Plus he knew the break-in would be on the news. The media were hungry for any kind of story related to Jack's murder. He set to work straightening things out in the office and studio, thankful that the burglar was a pro, not into destroying things for the sake of destruction. The office telephone rang. Not thinking, he picked it up before the machine answered, then hoped it wasn't another reporter.

"Is this Mr. Oscar Leopold?"

"Yes. The very same."

"I'm Maxine Dettling. I talked to your secretary last time I called, but now I have some additional information. I don't know why I didn't remember before, but I guess with Dr. Zucker's death and all, I was too mixed up."

"Could you refresh my memory about this again?" He had no idea who this woman was and had never heard of any Dr. Zucker. The closest Oscar had to a secretarial help was Sydney, and she hadn't told him about this woman calling. He lifted his office chair upright and sat down, locating a pen and pad of paper amid the desk clutter.

"Oh. Well, I worked for Dr. Zucker. The dentist? Yes. Well, when your secretary talked to me before, I told her the same thing I told the police. The fire that the doctor died in also destroyed all the x-rays, records and charts, including those of Mr. Gamble.

"But today I remembered that we had referred Mr. Gamble once to an oral surgeon. Do you know Dr. Vivian Orwell? To do a wisdom tooth extraction. I thought the information might help, because she would have X-rays, too."

"For the forensic identification?" Oscar was beginning to see what she was talking about.

"Yes. That's what the police wanted them for. But I guess they didn't need them after all. Anyway, I wanted to tell you that. You can tell the police, too, if you want."

"I'll do that. Thank you for calling."

He didn't see any great need to get the x-rays, but called the detective bureau and left the information for Detective Willis. He had asked Sydney to look into it, so maybe she forgot to tell him about calling the dentist, since it seemed like a dead end.

Later that afternoon, after the place was reassembled to its normal shambles, he decided to go on over to see Roy. He called first, having learned his lesson. Roy was at home. Alone this time.

Sydney had his keys, the last he knew. Surprisingly, her door was open when he went downstairs. She was working at the computer.

"Sydney, did you call a dentist about Big Jack's x-rays? And have you got my keys? I'm going out."

"The dentist is dead and his office burned down. Are you taking the Mustang? Because I might want to borrow it later." She didn't look away from the computer screen and kept clicking away at the keyboard. The printer was spitting out paper.

"Ha. You wish. In fact, we need to cover it up again. I don't want those tangerines eating up the finish with their citric acid. What are you doing?"

"Making you another copy of the computer information that got lifted." She picked up his keys off the table and tossed them to him.

"Really? That's great. I didn't think we had any after we sent the computer back."

"Well, we did. I had downloaded it onto my cloud backup—that's Internet storage if you don't know. Whoever stole your safe went to a whole lot of trouble for nothing. And by the way, don't you think it was ill-advised to give back the computer? I mean, if you're interested in defending Roy, a little missing evidence would help, wouldn't it?" She leaned back in her chair, put her feet up, and clasped her hands behind her head. She now had black eye shadow heavily applied around her eyes. A sort of a Marilyn Manson look.

"Sure. I could have, but it's illegal and unethical."

"So is breaking into the office and taking it in the first place."

"Not really. I was let in by an employee. And I was only borrowing the computer. I did send it back, you know. And you were the one who kicked in the door."

She raised her eyebrows, stood, and handed him a new flash drive and printout.

"Try and hang onto this one."

Oscar then made the mistake of answering the front door buzzer and had to spend nearly an hour listening to a young woman who wanted to be a new client. She had won one hundred thousand dollars on a scratch-off lottery instant ticket and was upset when she only ended up with twelve thousand. After the state held out money for the IRS, they claimed an additional chunk for a tax lien filed during her first marriage. The problem was, she said, that she had already signed a contract for a thirty-thousand dollar pickup truck and now didn't have enough money. Wasn't there something he could do? He referred her to an acquaintance who practiced tax law and sent her home.

Chapter Twenty-eight

"I see two big problems. First, these aren't all my cases," Roy said as he scanned the list.

"Some are. But most are Big Jack's. I don't know why my name is on these. The second problem might just be a mistake. The settlement amounts here can't be right." He ran a line with a red marker under one data line. "This is one of mine, I recognize the names of plaintiff and defendant. But the settlement amount is about four times what I settled the case for. See where it says two hundred eighty-five thousand?" He jabbed the pen into the figure. "I settled this for just shy of seventy-five grand. The client got two thirds after expenses and our cut, so she walked away with about fifty K and her hospital costs. This picture isn't right." Roy leaned back in his office chair, eyes running the columns of numbers.

"Another thing. I know for a fact that several of these, that were Jack's personal cases, ended up with no settlement at all to speak of. Two of these clients in particular, this Grubbs one for instance, kept coming around the office. I talked to him once when Jack wasn't available, and from his file there was nothing we could do for him. He just didn't have a case, and Jack settled it for the nuisance value. About five thousand. But according to this the case settled for a hundred-fifty thousand. It doesn't add up. Plus, here it's listed as my case."

Oscar sat in the side chair next to Roy's home office desk in his small den. He ran the possibilities through his head. It could be a mistake, but not likely. Certainly Roy would know which cases were his, so that part wasn't in error. It could be somebody trying to set him up, making him look responsible for the hidden settlements and payoffs, if that's what they were.

"Why would anyone in the office falsify the records?" Oscar asked. They adjourned to the kitchen table, drinking the coffee that was now ready. Oscar liked sugar in his, but all Roy had was honey. Honey wasn't sugar.

Roy got up and paced. He was wiping his face again and sweating. It wasn't hot in the kitchen. He had his suit coat off and his shirt sleeves rolled up.

"Somebody's trying to frame me. Maybe the real killer. I want to show you something I found. Come on back into the den."

"Don't you have air conditioning in this suburban palace?" Oscar asked.

"It gives me a headache."

Oscar followed him in. Roy went to his PC, turned it on, reached up to the top shelf of his bookcase, and pulled out a *Black's Law Dictionary*. He removed a flash drive from inside a space where he had hollowed out several pages. He inserted it in the computer and brought it up onto the screen.

"I see you finally found a use for that dictionary." Oscar had given it to him as a law school graduation present.

"Yeah. I cut the centers out of the last thirty pages so I can use it for a makeshift safe. Just enough space for a bundle of bills or something like this. I found it in Jack's safe deposit box today. You knew I was working on his estate for Lucy? I thought I might find cash, jewels, rare stamps, or something like that in the box, but there was only the deed to his condo, some old insurance policies and this flash drive. But it's encrypted, and I didn't have the password. Do you have it?"

Oscar remembered Sydney's password discovery. "Try Bigjack1957."

Roy punched it in and the computer accepted it. He looked at Oscar quizzically.

"Sydney." Oscar said.

A screen shot displayed that was similar to the one on the drive Oscar brought with him. Similar but not identical.

"What does this look like to you?" Roy asked.

It was a list like the one Oscar had gotten from the office computer. But this only contained a few cases with Roy listed as attorney and contained additional information. He scrolled down. There was a list of dates, amounts paid, case numbers, and the payees, with their foreign bank names and account numbers. Most of the names of the payees were either Timothy Bascomb or Robert Jerome Walters.

"It looks like what everyone is looking for. Proof of the insurance scam Jack was working. "

"Do you think Jack was using this for blackmail?" Roy asked.

"Doesn't make sense. He would only be implicating himself. He couldn't turn it over to the cops. Maybe it was his protection. These characters are not adverse to violence. Maybe this was his life insurance policy. If he died they would be fingered."

"If it was meant as insurance it didn't work." Roy said.

"Unless the killer didn't know of this particular copy. Or unless the other attorneys weren't involved in the killings. Maybe Jack was getting greedy, wanting a bigger share, and used the information as leverage." Oscar sat on the edge of the desk.

"So you're saying they wouldn't have killed him if they knew this existed."

"Probably not. Unless they thought they could get their hands on it. Maybe they thought they had all the records, killed him, then discovered the ones they got were fakes. The real question is, why do his office computer records, the fakes, have your name all over them?"

"Could be Jack's doing. He may have been trying to frame me. Cover himself if he got caught. But regardless of whether my name was on them or Jack's, they still pointed to the other attorneys involved. So whoever it was, they would want all of both versions."

"Could Jack have known about you and Lucy?"

"No. If he did, he would have done something more violent about it. He wasn't very subtle." Roy bummed a cigarette, and they stepped outside into the Florida room. There was a nice breeze coming through the screen. Next door, the neighbor, a thin white-haired retiree wearing a pale green polyester pants suit and white athletic shoes, was watering her flower boxes with a red plastic watering can. She had on headphones and was bouncing to the silent music as she worked.

"How do you think this all worked?" Oscar asked.

"I imagine they could have gotten together on certain of the bigger cases and agreed to maximum settlements, even where the facts wouldn't justify it. Who would complain? The insurance company gets rid of a litigation case, Jack gets his cut, and the insurance defense attorneys get an under-the-table bonus."

"Except that the insurance companies paid out more than they would have ordinarily. And in some cases it looks like the clients got only a fraction of what they should have gotten."

"Right. But the insurance companies accept the recommendation of their attorneys, who put up just enough fight and do just enough work on the case to make it look legitimate, then lay down and play dead and agree to a big settlement, which they then get a kickback on. And the clients never really know. The settlement checks go to the lawyer, and the lawyer writes the client a separate check for his share. It would be easy enough to make a fake release for the client to sign with a lower amount then forge his signature on the fake one with the higher amount."

"But the numbers here are pretty big. This represents a lot of cases."

"We handled a lot of cases," Roy said. "Our television ads run state-wide. We have our Miami satellite office. Most importantly there's the referral system that allows us to pay a referral fee to any lawyer in the state that sends us a case. For the referring attorney, it's a good deal. He gets one-third of the fee for doing nothing. Until Jack's death we were pulling in about three new quality cases a week plus a half-dozen or so arguable ones. Jack got the best ones. Divided between the rest of us and Jack, that's a good caseload. And nearly all of Jack's settled. If you figure his are settling for even 25 percent above what they're worth and none come back no-cause, plus screwing some of the clients out of their share, and you're talking a lot of additional money."

"Enough to kill for."

"Sure. But why would the insurance attorneys kill him? He was their meat and potatoes," Roy said.

Oscar wondered about Roy's speculation. Oscar hadn't ruled out Lucy, disgruntled clients like Billy Grubbs and especially Cake, or even Roy himself. Enough to kill for if Jack had been socking huge amounts of money away somewhere and the killer thought it could be reached. Or already had it. Did Roy have it?

"Unless he was going to get caught and wanted to take them down with him. But what about the bar association. Wouldn't they be able to check a client's complaint?" Oscar asked.

"Sure. A full-blown investigation by the Bar Association grievance committee would probably have revealed the whole scheme. They could audit his trust account if they want and probably would. It would have been crazy for him to pull something like that and take a chance on getting caught."

"Unless he was planning on skipping town anyway."

"Could be. But he didn't get far did he? And Lucy says there isn't any stash of cash she knows about."

"Unless she's in on it or Jack hid it, planning on dumping her too."

Roy answered quickly. "I don't think so. So now what do we do?"

"I think what you have here is a hot potato. We should probably turn it over to the Attorney General's office. Maybe the FBI for a racketeering investigation. There's bound to be some kind of federal violation here. Maybe mail fraud, for instance. The question is, will this clear you? I don't think giving it up right now will help your case at all. They may still think you killed him. Or that you were involved in the scam. Or that you fabricated this version of the data. Maybe there are other versions or the whole thing is fabricated." Oscar was thinking aloud.

"Probably our best course of action is to let out word that we have this. Use it for bait and leverage. Walters already knows we had it, at least the version implicating you, but I don't know for sure if he was working with Bascomb over in Apalachicola. It's possible they don't know about each other. The information on this could very well have been involved in the reason for Jack's death," Oscar said.

He studied Roy carefully. He appeared tired, and his complexion was sallow—definitely not a healthy look. Oscar worried that Roy's new smoking habit, combined with the obesity and stress, might do him in. But he had to find out more, even if it meant just a smidgen more stress. Oscar went to the bathroom and jettisoned one of the beers he'd been drinking. When he came back Roy was sitting on a bar stool in the kitchen.

"Now don't get mad, but I have to ask you another question. And I want you to be straight with me."

Roy stubbed out his cigarette in a coffee cup.

"What?" He looked at Oscar warily.

"Do you think Lucy could have worked with someone else to plan Jack's death? Someone whom she might have been involved with maybe? There are signs pointing that way."

"You mean someone like me?"

"Not necessarily you. Maybe somebody else. Do you think she could have carried it off all by herself?"

Roy was up again, patting his pockets for Oscar's cigarettes he had left in the den.

"I don't know. I gently asked if she did it, and she denied it. I think she's the only one who could have done it, but can't imagine who might have helped her. I can tell you honestly that I didn't do it. She said she knew Jack was having an affair with someone. Wouldn't tell me who. I knew it was working around in her, even though she was seeing me.

"Funny, isn't it that she was cheating on him but didn't want him cheating on her? She said she could arrange to take care of things if she wanted. Doing it all alone, though, I can't say. She's not very big, and Jack was huge. She did possess the temperament for it, though. My gut is that she did it alone. But I have no irrefutable proof that she was definitely involved with someone else. Just circumstantial."

"The kind, absent your impending confession, that they have against you."

"Right. But if someone else was involved, I guess I don't know what to do. I suppose it's a good thing I didn't already plead guilty."

"When is Lucy supposed to get the insurance money?"

"On Friday. She's meeting the insurance adjuster at his office at nine."

"When does she have access to the funds?"

"Immediately. I arranged for a bank draft. It's as good as cash."

"Do you have any plans when the money comes in?" Oscar wondered what could be done with two and a half million dollars. Lots of things.

"It's not my money, Oscar."

"I know. I meant do you know if Lucy had any plans."

"You mean like leaving town? She wouldn't leave without me, and I can't leave the state, of course, because of the bond, but Lucy plans a short trip to the islands. She says she needs to get away and I agree. She's gone through a lot lately."

"The Bahamas?"

"Yes. Freeport. Just for a week or so. She says she's running over on her boat. Why? Do you seriously think she might skip?"

"I don't know. But if she's the guilty one we can't have you left here holding the bag. That's not the kind of commitment you bargained for."

Oscar took both flash drives with him, trying to decide where to keep them until Sydney could upload them on her cloud, whatever that was. Meanwhile, keep them in a safe place.

On his way back to the office a green panel van began tailgating his Toyota. It was so close to his bumper he could see only the grill and headlights in his rear view mirror and the chrome FORD letters in reverse. He sped up, but it stayed with him and even rammed him lightly once, throwing his head back into the headrest. He was worried that it might be a bump and rob about to happen. Usually the local thugs played the game on cars with out-of-state plates. They bump the car then rob the trusting tourists when they pull over to check the damage and exchange insurance information. Even if the bad guys got caught, the tourists often would not return to testify at a trial. More likely it was Rico or one of his goons, not happy with what they found in the safe.

The traffic was light, but there was no hope that the Toyota could outrun the big truck. Oscar was amazed that anyone would be so brazen to try running him off the road with it still being daylight. Cops could be anywhere. And looking at his car, it was hard to believe any thief would believe there was anything inside worth stealing, so it had to be something personal.

He made a hard right, giving the worn shocks and tires on the Toyota a workout, praying that the tires wouldn't pop right then. The van skidded around the corner behind him, careening off the front fender of a parked car near the corner. The little Toyota wasn't too fast but was pretty maneuverable. He was downshifting around the corners and accelerating out of the turns like he had done as a kid, experimenting after just getting his driving license.

He made two more quick turns and gained a little ground, then cut through a gas station and got out onto Dixie Highway. He could see the van coming up fast in the left lane. The twenty-five semi-automatic was still in the glove box. He reached over and got it, thankful now that the glove box lock was broken.

He pulled the slide back, chambering a round, flicked off the safety, rolled down the window the rest of the way and waited for the van to come up alongside. There was a light coming up. It turned yellow and was still a half block ahead. Then red. The traffic on the cross street was just entering the intersection when he and the van sped through. He heard, more than saw, cars screeching and sliding into each other as they careened through.

The right front fender of the van was just to his left, veering toward him. The Toyota was shuddering with the unaccustomed speed, and the steering wheel vibrated in his hands. The traffic ahead was clear and Oscar was going sixty-five, about the top limit for the worn-out little car. He reached across his body with his right hand and put three quick shots into the Ford's fender, not really aiming and missing the tire.

It was enough.

The driver overreacted, hitting his brakes or throwing it into reverse, Oscar didn't know which. But the van jerked hard, nearly stopping, and spun like someone had thrown a giant speed bump up in front of it. Then it tipped over on its side and slid, throwing a shower of sparks up and making a horrendous squeal. Oscar didn't wait to see if the driver was okay.

He slowed, turned at the next corner and made his way home on the side streets, trying to calm his pounding heart. Chase scenes weren't nearly so much fun in person as they looked in the movies. He pulled in behind his building and rested his head on his arms on the steering wheel. Then realized he still held the pistol. He dropped it onto the passenger seat. His heart hadn't slowed. He remembered that his father had died of a heart attack at sixty-three, and his grandfather at only forty-seven. Oscar had dropped out of full-time law to avoid the stress. Now look at me, he thought.

In less than a week he had fired a gun at someone twice. That was, he understood, the purpose of handguns, but he had never done it before. The gun should be cleaned, he thought. He took it inside and up to his apartment, then remembered the flash drive. He put it in the pocket of his old golf bag, took it outside and locked the clubs in the trunk of the Mustang.

After cleaning the pistol, reloading it, and mixing himself a gin and tonic, Oscar tried to decide if he should call the cops to report the van. It shouldn't be hard to find. But the way his luck was going nowadays and his reputation with Sheila, he would probably be facing another firearms charge.

Who could it have been? After some reflection, Oscar dismissed the idea that it was run-of-the-mill criminals. His beater of a Toyota didn't hold out the promise of anyone with cash inside and they wouldn't want the car. So that left someone singling him out. Attorney Walters had given him three days; had he changed his mind? He could call and ask. Maybe it was friends of the guy he had shot the first time or it might be whoever else might have killed Jack. It could be he was getting too close to someone.

Lucy was looking better as a suspect all the time.

Oscar was beat, so he unplugged the telephone, turned off his cell, and decided to hide out inside, get some rest, and start fresh in the morning. There was half a pizza from the distant past in the freezer. He called it and two beers dinner. He fell asleep fully dressed, sitting up in bed, and dreamt of guns, and cars, and walking naked through his old high school.

Chapter Twenty-nine

Sydney had taped a sign on the front door of the gallery advising delivery people to ring the buzzer for entry. It also said that Mr. Leopold had moved out of town until midsummer to discourage the news reporters. But the buzzer was ringing and had been ringing long enough for him to realize it wasn't part of his dream. He swung his feet over the side of the bed, knocking over what was left of his drink from the night before.

The buzzer stopped. He stumbled to the bathroom, stepping on the wedge of lime from the drink. It was nearly eight. He hoped eight in the morning and not evening. The buzzer resumed just as he was stripping for a shower. From the balcony Oscar called down. "Who's down there and what the hell is so important?"

"I have a delivery for you."

"Leave it by the door. I'll get it in a while."

"No, you have to sign." An attractive woman in her twenties with close-cropped blonde hair, wearing shorts, walking shoes, and a short blue jacket came into view and looked up. She held up a sheaf of papers at him.

"Okay. Be right down." He pulled on his pants and tried not to fall down the stairs. Too much activity before his shower and coffee. Oscar relied on his morning ritual to fully wake up. This included two cups of coffee and CNN Headline News.

There was no package visible with the young woman. He unlocked the door and opened it, but she wouldn't come in.

"Are you Mr. Oscar Leopold?"

"That's me." He hoped she wasn't armed.

"This is for you." She handed him the papers she had waved before, then turned to leave.

"Wait a minute. What is this?" He was holding the door handle in one hand and the papers in the other.

"I don't read them. I just serve them." She walked quickly away.

Oscar scanned them.

He was being sued.

By the guy Sanchez, whom he had shot, and by one of his friends who had been there. Other than in his divorce, Oscar had never been a participant in a lawsuit. He read the pleadings. Civil assault, battery, false imprisonment, permanent disability, emotional distress—it went on and on. He looked at the demand at the end. They wanted twenty million. Good luck with that. Oscar didn't know the lawyer for the plaintiffs. Must be some new hotshot who hadn't heard the term judgment-proof. He tossed the papers on his desk and went back upstairs to start over.

Oscar needed a break. Events had been just too much lately. He hadn't had time to work on his sculpture or do much else other than play detective. The gallery show was ready to go, so he spent the morning with Sydney mailing out the invitations and press releases and made a quick call to the artist confirming her attendance at the opening in two weeks. She was going to drive all the way from Chicago. Oscar offered to let her stay with him, but she said she had a friend in the area and was driving down with her husband. She stressed the husband. He made a note to call a maid service to clean the gallery and wash the big display windows.

Lucy was to get the insurance money on Friday. Oscar's pretrial was coming up in a week on Tuesday. Roy's arraignment was set for a week from Thursday. There was only one day left on attorney Walters' deadline—if it was still in effect since the break-in.

Too many issues to deal with.

The telephone started to ring just as he was locking up and getting ready to go out. He considered letting the voicemail get it but hurried back inside. He picked it up on the fifth ring.

"Hello?" he said, just a bit out of breath from the short run. Maybe he should do some kind of exercise, after all.

"Is this attorney Leopold?"

"Yes, who's calling?"

"This is Laurie Small from Channel Three Action News. Do you plan on pleading Mr. Flagler guilty?"

He hung the telephone up. It almost immediately rang again.

"I have no comment," Oscar said, picking up again.

"Excuse me? Is this Mr. Leopold's office?" It was a different person.

"Yes. Sorry. Are you a reporter?"

"No, I'm not. Will you hold for attorney Carl Seacomb?"

"Sure."

Seacomb. He was another of the defense lawyers involved in the scam. Hadn't heard from him yet.

"Mr. Leopold?"

"Yup."

"My name is Carl Seacomb, as you know, and I'm calling from Miami. I understand from some associates that you're defending Roy Flagler, accused of murdering Jack Gamble."

"That's right."

"I thought we might get together to discuss matters of mutual interest. Wherever you like and at your convenience of course."

"You don't have a limousine waiting outside do you?"

"A limousine? I'm afraid I don't know what you mean."

"Never mind. The thing is, I'm kind of busy right now. I suggest you call Robert Walters. He can probably fill you in on the problem you have."

"What problem is that?"

"I think we both know why you called. I have the information you all need in a safe place and copies with people who will know what to do with it if anything happens to me. Now I have to run."

"You're a very confusing man Mr. Leopold, or perhaps just confused. I will call you back in a few days. Now don't get paranoid. I merely want to discuss the situation that I believe could easily be misinterpreted if not explained properly. Things need to be kept in their proper context."

"Yeah, yeah, yeah. Bye." He hung up. At this point he could see no reason to talk to another of the involved attorneys. Oscar figured they were running scared, not knowing who had what information on them and afraid of the consequences of public disclosure. When you threaten someone's livelihood they tend to get nervous and unpredictable. He sure didn't need another experience like the one with Walters.

On the other hand it would be helpful to know whether the defense lawyers were working together on the scam or if Big Jack had separate deals with each of them. Seacomb was a wild card. Oscar decided to let him stew a little, then call him for information later.

Chapter Thirty

Oscar found Detective Willis back of the station house putting his golf clubs into the trunk of his car, a late model two-door black Buick Regal. He slammed the trunk and pretended not to see Oscar, but Oscar caught up to him before he got the driver's door closed. He was wearing bright red slacks, a striped polo shirt, and a white golf cap. Not detective attire. It must be his day off.

Oscar had known Willis since his first days at the public defender's office. In a sense they grew up together in their respective occupations. They had a cordial relationship, and had even played poker every Wednesday night over one winter with a group of other cops. When Oscar dropped out of the legal business, they hadn't kept up the relationship. Willis had been fond of Oscar's ex-wife Pam and still thought Oscar was a jerk for leaving her.

"Willis! Wait a second. Did you get my message?" He ran up and put his hand on Willis' car door. Willis looked up at Oscar with a pained expression, one foot still on the pavement.

"Taking off early to play a little golf, eh?"

"Good guess."

"Looks like a good day for it. Do you always keep your clubs here at the office?"

"Okay. Say what you came here to say. It'll take sixty seconds for the car interior cool off. I can't wait longer than that, so make it fast." Willis had worked twelve days without a day off and was anxious for a little relaxation. The last thing he needed was Leopold making him continue his workday.

"You should know better than to buy a black car in this climate."

"I got a deal on it. My brother in Philly. Now what do you want?"

"Did you check on that information about the dental x-rays on Jack Gamble?"

"I got the message, went over and got the x-rays myself and took them to forensics. They should have an answer for me Friday morning. But it's just a formality. I doubt that we need any additional evidence. The wife identified the body. There was physical evidence. DNA evidence. Everything matched up. We even matched the hair samples on the body with hair from his brush at his home. I don't think you're giving me anything new."

"I'm just doing my job. Covering all the bases. I met with Cake, you remember? The client?"

"I remember. So?"

"Do you think he was involved?"

"We have the guy who was involved. Your client, remember? But I checked out Cake myself. He was playing bingo at St. Luke's when the murder went down. Besides which, I don't think he has the brains to pull the job off without blowing himself up too."

"He told me he was at the clinic with an infection."

"He was playing bingo."

"What about Billy Grubbs?"

"The other client? Disappeared. But while he would have been a potential suspect if we didn't have Flagler, all he has is motive. No means, no opportunity, and no evidence whatsoever that he was involved. His girlfriend said he leaves town for weeks at a time and comes back stinking drunk and broke. I expect the same thing will happen this time. So is that all? I have an appointment."

"One more thing. What if the dental doesn't match up?"

Willis put his foot in the car and started the engine, leaning over to flip the air conditioner to high. He took the golf cap off, exposing his close cropped Marine hair cut.

"How many three hundred fifty pound middle-aged guys wearing Gamble's clothes, jewelry, and his hair with an exact DNA match do you think there could have been on that boat." He shook his head in disgust, pulled the door out from under Oscar's arm, and pulled away.

Chapter Thirty-one

Wednesday morning. Oscar decided he had to secure the flash drives and printouts in a safe place, at least for a few days. Sydney had uploaded them, but there was the real possibility that the information could be lost if something happened to her. He felt more comfortable with something tangible that could be turned over to the police when the time came. The time limit he'd been given by Walters was worrying him. He thought of hiding them under his mattress, or in the freezer, or the side pocket of his golf bag, but these all seemed a bit lame. While his safe deposit box at Barnett Bank was secure, it could also be ordered sealed by the courts, and Oscar knew the power and influence wielded by big law firms like that of Walters.

He took the drive downtown to the post office and sent it in an Express Mail pouch along with the hard copy of data made by Sydney and addressed the package to himself. He would have to sign for it to get delivery. The security of the postal service was backed by the federal government, and who was going to interfere with that? It seemed safer to him for a day or two in the hands of the post office than it was in the car or his office. Turning it over to the police or State's Attorney seemed a bad idea until he found out whether it was legitimate.

He then verified with the clerk that the first delivery attempt would be Thursday but if he was not there they would attempt redelivery on Friday. If he still wasn't there to sign for it, they would hold it at the post office for three days. If it wasn't picked up, it would be returned to sender at Roy's address.

Back home, Sydney was checking her secure email.

The email was clearly from Rico. She didn't think he had any idea of her relationship with Oscar, so his new request to get Lucy's cooperation in any way necessary was a serious conflict of interest. It looked like she was going to have to come clean with Oscar. For his own safety. She had never told anyone. How would he react? Could she tell him part of what she'd done without making him freak? She didn't think of herself as a bad person. Certainly not a sociopath. But the fact was she felt no remorse or guilt for the things she'd done. Even for the killings. They were all bad people who had done bad things that they were never called on. She didn't think of herself as a superhero, a Paladin, or crusader for justice. It was a service business. Kind of a social service agency. She had to either tell him or leave him. Leaving would be hard but telling might cause him to leave her.

She had to be ready to move quickly if the confession to Oscar didn't go well. She didn't need the computer since her files were all encrypted and password protected on the cloud storage which she could access from anywhere. Guns were always available, especially in the south. Thank God for the gun shows. The money, though, would have to be packed and either shipped or hand-carried. It was mostly hundreds and not as bulky as she would have thought. She stuffed it in her backpack. It only weighed about seventeen pounds. A lot of money for such a small package. She put the backpack in the wall space and replaced the panel. The only other thing she would take would be a change of clothes and personal hygiene items. Everything else could be replaced. She hoped it wouldn't come to that.

She saved an encrypted copy of the message on another remote website and didn't respond to either email. She had to get Oscar alone for awhile. Explain things and see if the pieces held together when she dropped them on the floor.

Chapter Thirty-two

Early the next morning she talked Oscar into a day trip. A chance to relax, unwind, take a day without talking about the case. Breakfast at the marina on the Intracoastal was the first stop. Then they walked out to see the boats. Tourists liked to come down and walk the docks, taking pictures and looking at the boats. The sun was in full Florida force, and just a few high skinny clouds painted the sky.

The wood of the dock was weathered gray, and they could see the water below through the narrowly spaced planks. There was a strong fish smell at low tide, with the oysters, seaweed, and barnacles near shore exposed.

"What a stink," Sydney said.

"I like it. The essence of the sea. It's alive."

"Smells like it's dead to me"

Several big trawlers were moored on their left, while narrower docks shot off to the right to accommodate a variety of deep-sea charter sport fishing boats.

One had just come in from an overnight trip, and two sun-burned, middle-aged fishermen appearing slightly drunk were attempting to climb back on the dock from the deck of the boat carrying a large tarpon between them. He was surprised, since most of the charter boats made their clients release the tarpon they caught. They were inedible anyway, so what was the point? Probably planning on having it mounted for their office wall.

What they didn't know was that taxidermists typically used a hand colored plastic mount and threw the actual fish away. Reputable charter captains explained this to the client, released the fish after photos, then would steer the client to a "release mount" that they would sell to them.

They turned back toward the fishermen when they heard the yelling of the crowd, then the sounds of someone thrashing around in the water. One drunken fisherman had indeed fallen in. The other was spread-eagled on the fish trying to keep it from slipping into the water. The crowd applauded and cheered as the fish slid into the water, leaving a chagrined and slimy fisherman with a story to tell. The boat captain, looking completely disgusted, was throwing a line to the guy.

Oscar let her drive, not that he had much choice. Sydney loved the Mustang almost as much as he did. Not quite as much since he loved it enough to not let himself drive it too often. She would hardly have ever been out of it had it been hers. They headed up to Cape Canaveral. There was a restaurant in Cocoa Village on the mainland that served terrific stone crab claws as part of a seafood plate that Oscar loved.

They pretended to be tourists. He bought her T-shirts, they visited a shell shop, and she nearly made the turn west on County Road 520 to go to Disney World when his good sense prevailed.

After dinner they walked the narrow streets of Cocoa, window shopping and talking. The little downtown area with its two-story brick and block storefronts reminded Oscar of many such small towns in the Midwest, though the architecture was unusual for Florida. Artists had taken over many of the upper floors, and there were several galleries sprinkled through the few short blocks. No doubt the artists would be forced out by high rents when the area was eventually discovered by the fashionable set and the developers who attended them.

Sydney thought now was a good time to talk. They were sitting on a bench in a small park in front of a fountain in the center of town. It was shady and cool.

"There's something you need to know about me."

Oscar crushed his newly lit cigarette with his shoe and turned to face her.

"What, you're pregnant?"

She bumped shoulders with him. "No, you ass. This is serious. I know we weren't going to talk about the case, but this relates to it and you need to know everything for your own safety as well as Roy's."

He started to say something, and she held her palm up to face him.

"Let me finish. Then you can ask questions or call the police, or just leave. Bascomb didn't commit suicide. Rico killed him, I tried to stop him, but I was too late. I had the chance to kill Rico, but I didn't. Too risky. You need to know I've killed people before. Bad people who deserved it. But still. There it is."

Until now she didn't know what a stunned look was. Oscar's mouth had actually dropped open and he stared blankly at her, as if wondering if this was a joke or a confession. "You killed people? Intentionally?"

"Oscar, I wasn't entirely truthful to you when we first met. Okay— I lied my ass off. I originally came from the New York-New Jersey area where I ran a business helping people who had nowhere to turn. It started out when I was young, seventeen. My little brother was abducted, raped and killed by a neighbor. The perp was arrested, tried, and convicted. That should have been the end of it but it was too much for mom. Dad had died two years before in a construction accident. Then this. She walked in front of a bus. Maybe it was an accident. Then the guy appealed his conviction, and it got thrown out on a technicality. Prosecutorial misconduct, they said. So he was free. I blamed him for my brother and my mother. I couldn't stand that he was walking around like nothing had happened. So I did something about it. I followed him for days until, well, I got the opportunity to push him off the subway platform in front of a train. I expected to be arrested, but no one noticed what I did, they were so focused on him falling and the train zooming by. So I got away with it, and it felt good."

Oscar was silent for a moment, searching her face. She stared at him, almost defiant. "Sydney, I can't even say that's morally wrong. Illegal yes, but the right thing to do, most would agree. Well, not the police."

"That's not all. Here I was, just a kid. No parents, no income. I had the apartment but no way to pay for it. But I did have a computer and knew how to use it. So I decided to see if I could help other people who needed justice. I set up my website, offering to solve problems. I wasn't out to be a hired killer, but there were things that I could do to help that didn't necessarily involve killing. I did things anonymously, to help people, and got paid for it.

"My first case was a plea for help from a woman out in Queens. Her repeated calls to the police were ignored. A bad neighbor had been bullying her kids, partying late into the night with his outlaw friends, had a vicious dog, was stealing newspapers, the list went on and on. The original email was almost a short story in itself. I sent her an email request for a cash deposit to be sent to a post office box I'd opened. She sent the money. It was only a thousand dollars, but was a lot to me. I checked out the neighbor and decided I couldn't confront him directly. Back then I didn't know martial arts and had no firearm training, so what to do? Then I had an idea and solved the problem. The client emailed me the next day saying that she didn't need my help any more since the client's house had burned down. She didn't ask for a refund, so I think she understood what happened."

"What about Bascomb and Rico?" Oscar wasn't smiling any longer and lit another cigarette.

"I've continued to run the same business from here, though it's a lot more sophisticated now. Lots of firewalls. I was originally contacted through my website by Rico to kill Big Jack. I didn't take the case, but Rico had already sent the money. A lot of it. He wouldn't take a refund and threatened to go after those he called my friends, which meant you, since you are the only friend I have." She looked at him, tears welling up. He patted her arm. She wiped her eyes.

"He demanded that I carry out another hit to earn the money I'd taken. I was reluctant, but after I learned what scum Bascomb was, I decided to look into it on our trip to Apalachicola. Rico wasn't supposed to be there, but when I saw him walk into Bascomb's office my gut told me why. I hesitated, conflicted, and when I finally decided to try to stop Rico, it was too late. I warned him off, but he's a real danger since he knows who I am and what I look like. Which means he might know about you. You could be in danger because of me. That's all. So now my fate is yours." She turned and stared at the fountain.

"Are you going to keep this up? This business of yours?"

"I don't know."

Oscar stood.

"I'm sure I'll have lots of questions as time goes on. I'm not turning you in. I should. But we had something special once and as far as I'm concerned it's still there. I have to digest all this. You're trying to do what you think is right. Helping people. Killing others. I can't say that's something I could do, except in self defense, but I haven't sat in your chair so I'm not judging. Let's take it a day at a time, sort everything out with Roy, Rico, and the cops and see where it all ends up."

Sydney jumped up and grabbed him in a fierce hug. He could feel her tears wetting his shirt.

They decided against spending the night in Cocoa, went back to the gallery and sat on the balcony talking until early morning. Oscar was enjoying the comfortable feeling of spending a lot of time with someone he really cared about. He had been relationship-shy since the divorce and, while he wasn't ready to call it a commitment quite yet, he wasn't averse to the notion. And living alone wasn't his idea of living well. He hoped she would come around to his feelings about their relationship.

Oscar had just finished cleaning the kitchen when Sydney came running up the stairs. She was carrying one of her black automatic rifles in both hands across her chest.

"You got company, Oscar!" she said quickly, but quietly in her hoarse voice. She ran to the front window and peered out from the side, pulling the slide back on the gun to load it for firing as she watched.

"What's up?" Oscar wiped his hands on his pants, deciding whether he should find a gun fast. The image of cavalry soldiers manning the stockade fort in the old West came to mind.

"The limo's back. And Rico and another guy are headed this way."

Oscar looked out the window. Sure enough, the limo was parked on the street opposite the building, and the two men, this time wearing sunglasses, were coming toward his front door.

"What do we do?" Sydney asked.

"How about we go out the back?" While he was confident Sydney could take them both out, he had always believed that if an escape route was available the best thing to do was take it. Flight rather than fight.

The door buzzer and the telephone rang at the same time.

"This is probably that Walters guy again. Stand by for the time being. Ignore the door." He answered the telephone while Sydney ran toward the stairs. Oscar hoped she wasn't going to open fire.

"Mr. Leopold. This is Robert Jerome Walters."

"Why am I not surprised? Are you planning to strip me down again? I think you get your kicks that way."

Sydney looked up the stairs at Oscar questioningly.

"No need to get personal, Mr. Leopold. And I apologize for the unpleasantness of the other day. I called to invite you to lunch."

"I think I've had enough of your hospitality. And I've already eaten. Thanks anyway."

"You will recall our previous conversation perhaps? The deadline?"

"I know it's expired. And my impression was you already have what you wanted." Oscar wondered whether this would be a good time to ask for the fifty thousand.

"Not exactly. But I wanted to talk to you about another option. One that could prove even more beneficial to you.

Could we meet for a short talk? Perhaps somewhere where you would feel more comfortable. I have a car available. You name the place."

"I have my own car. And I drive it myself. But I could meet with you briefly. How about in the park across from the police station downtown in three hours? We can sit and talk, just the two of us, on the bench near the fountain."

"Very well. But I want to assure you that you have nothing to fear from me at this point, Mr. Leopold."

"That remains to be seen."

By the time he got downstairs, no one was at the door, and the limo was gone.

Chapter Thirty-three

Sydney was in the Toyota parked alongside the street with a clear view of the park across from the police entrance. She sat in the shade of a jacaranda tree, and its lilac-like flower petals were drifting down onto the car with the light breeze. Oscar had a new transmitter "bug" on, and Sydney had hooked a recorder up to the receiver in the car. They still hoped to get some kind of admission that might help clear Roy. Oscar had arrived second, driving separately in the Mustang, hoping not to tip off anyone watching that Sydney was already there. A lone unoccupied patrol car stood at the front curb in front of the police station. A few people walked in the park, taking relief from the sun under the trees, but the bench a few yards off the sidewalk that he had suggested to Walters was empty. Oscar decided to wear a blue blazer, though the temperature had climbed to eighty-five. All the better to hide his .32 automatic.

He didn't really think Walters would try anything violent in broad daylight, but he had been surprised before. Nervous and perspiring, he had to hold himself back from getting up and walking away. His stomach was in knots, and he felt the beginnings of a headache in the tension at the back of his neck as he sat on the bench and tried to look at ease. Maybe he should have brought a newspaper.

The Cadillac limo pulled up. The driver let Walters out, then drove a half block down the street and waited, leaving the engine and the air conditioning running. Walters was dressed as if he was going into federal court, a slick black Armani suit, five-hundred dollar shoes, a white silk handkerchief in his breast pocket. He stepped carefully across the grass, as if avoiding dog excrement, and sat next to Oscar after first brushing invisible dust from the seat of the bench.

"You didn't happen to bring the computer information with you, by any chance? And I mean the correct ones, not the doctored ones we received earlier." His eyes were on the police station.

"You stole the only information I had, the flash drive and printouts. Now what's up? Someone tried to kill me. You seem to be the most likely suspect." Oscar hadn't taken his eyes off him.

Walters turned toward him then.

"Mr. Leopold, I'm surprised at you. I have no reason at this point to do harm to you. We may have need of each other. And I don't solve my problems by killing people. There are more civilized ways of solving problems. And we both know what I got from you before is not the whole of it."

"I hear your buddy Timmy Bascomb killed himself, but the police have questions." Oscar hoped for a reaction.

Nope.

"Who? Bascomb? I'm not acquainted with any Bascomb. Why would you think this person was a friend of mine?"

"You were both involved with the same insurance scam with Big Jack. It's pretty clear that there had to be some overlap. There were cases where you worked together. So cut the crap. What happened? Was Timmy going to cut a deal with the cops and rat you out, so you had to get rid of him like you did Big Jack?"

Walters smiled and put his hand on Oscar's arm. Oscar pulled away and looked to be sure it wasn't a signal and that no one was getting out of the limo.

"Slow down, Mr. Leopold. I can hardly keep up with your illogical leaps and conclusions. I certainly had nothing to do with anyone's death. If your Mr. Bascomb decided to end his life, that was a most personal decision he made on his own. I wasn't consulted nor involved. But what you're saying indicates that you do have the rest of the computer information. So why not discuss that.

"I'm willing to give you another option, as I said. You have seen the data. You must have an idea of the arrangement we had with Mr. Gamble."

"Who exactly is 'we'?" Oscar asked. He was hoping for names, places, and dates to verify the information on the disk. The taped recording could then be used against Walters.

"My associates, of course. We can discuss specifics later if we can come to an understanding. My proposal is this. You take over where Jack Gamble left off. Step into his shoes, as it were."

"You want me to take over his firm? Then do the same deals he was doing with you?"

"Exactly. Nothing illegal. I could not be a part of that. We like to have a personal relationship with those with whom we deal."

Oscar cursed silently. R.J. was covering himself in the event he was being recorded.

"I've had you checked out. You appear to be a more skilled attorney than Jack Gamble. We could probably do even better with you than we did with him. And you need the money. I will provide the funding for you to buy the firm's assets from his estate, a loan at a reasonable interest rate. You take over the caseload, the advertising, and the business relationship. Believe me, it will be lucrative. You would be on television." Walters grinned, displaying his expensive dental work.

Oscar couldn't help but glance over to where Sydney sat down the block recording all this. Television? He remembered the commercials run by Big Jack. Some were animated; others were of him standing in a courtroom pleading for people to call if they had been injured in any type of accident. It was one of the few occasions when Gamble had ever actually been in a courtroom. He begged them to call his 800 number, and then the scene cut away to him signing up a client in a hospital. One of his sales pitches was "don't get mad, and don't get even—get the money you deserve." It was all too sleazy for Oscar.

"Sorry, not interested. I'd have to stand on my head for the commercials, and I'm not that athletic. While I have no objection to *having* a lot of money, I don't want to have to do what it takes to *make* a lot of it. Especially what you're proposing I do. Seems like a conflict of interest for you, too. But I'd like to ask you a question while you're here. Just so I haven't wasted your time coming up here to see me."

"I'm not sure we have anything else to talk about." Walters had stood and signaled to the limo. "You have twenty-four hours more to get me the remaining computer information and satisfy me that there are no copies anywhere else. How you do that is up to you."

"Was Jack blackmailing you? Is that why you had him killed? Or did he just want out and you weren't about to let him go?"

Oscar stood and followed as Walters walked toward the limo that was moving slowly in reverse toward them. Another police car had pulled up across the street and the two officers sat inside, gathering their paperwork.

"That was probably it. You wouldn't let him out, so when he insisted and said he would use the computer information to protect himself, you had to get rid of him. But you counted on being able to retain control of the firm through making a new deal with Roy. When Roy was arrested for the murder, it threw your plans off. Now you have to have the evidence, or you and your buddies are fucked."

Walters was getting into the rear of the car, ignoring him.

"That's it, isn't it?" he yelled.

Walters closed the door. But the car sat still, and then the dark tinted rear window slid down. Oscar walked over to the curb. Walters got in the final word before he pulled away.

"I think that you will soon be surprised at how anxious you will be to help us. Everyone has a weak spot Mr. Leopold. If yours is not money then we shall see what it is."

Oscar looked across the street. The cops were still there and the one in the passenger seat was opening his door. They weren't looking in his direction, but he could easily get their attention.

"One more thing, R.J.,"

Walters leaned toward the open window again, looking at Oscar.

"I don't like being threatened."

He punched Walters square in the nose through the open window, using the left jab he had been proud of in high school, and stepped back. His knuckles hurt, and he hoped he hadn't dislocated one of them. He wiped the damp bloodiness from them on his slacks and waved to Sydney to bring the car up. The driver's door of the limo started to open, but Oscar heard a loud command from inside. The door closed as the limo pulled away.

Chapter Thirty-four

At three that afternoon the personal line in his apartment rang. Oscar half expected it to be Walters.

"Leopold?" the caller asked. It wasn't Walters, but Oscar didn't recognize the voice at first.

"That's me. Who is this?"

"I have your friend Roy Flagler with me." The caller paused for a moment. "He is your friend isn't he?"

"What are you talking about? Who are you?"

"Listen carefully," the caller said. He had a deep voice with a trace of a southern accent. It sounded familiar. The next voice on the line was Roy's.

"Oscar! You got to get me out of this one. These bastards are—" The line was pulled away from him. He sounded scared.

"So you recognize the voice, I take it?"

"What do you want?" Oscar remembered the voice now.

Rico laughed. "Really? You must be a lawyer. Now listen. I want the flash drives, or flash drive and any computers that were used to copy them. All of them. Come alone or your boy will be dead."

"I don't have what you want. But I can get it tomorrow."

Rico laughed again, an insane high pitched sort of laugh that caused Oscar to suspect the guy was on some kind of amphetamine.

"Don't bullshit me, Leopold. Do you really want to negotiate with his life? I convinced Flagler to tell me about the stuff he gave you."

"I'm not trying to stall. I just can't get my hands on them right now. They are out of reach until tomorrow."

"Shut up! I told you to listen. I'm only going to tell you this once. Out on County Road 721, the other side of Lake Okeechobee. You'll see a Survey Crew Ahead sign. There's a shack on the corner where an old woman sells boiled peanuts. Turn west on the sand road into the cane field and follow it about two hundred yards until you come to a clearing and a steel pole barn. I'll meet you there and exchange the computer stuff for your friend. Be there at six if you want to see them alive again. And come alone. If there are any police they die."

Rico had given the directions slowly, as if Oscar was writing them down. Then the line went dead.

Now what? Oscar didn't have the flash drive. He had secured it too well. And he was quite sure this was not planned to be a simple exchange. They could both end up dead or missing. He stood with the telephone still in his hand going over his options. The telephone began to talk to him, "If you want to make a call, please hang up." He hung up and went downstairs to find Sydney. He had three hours.

"How about if we give them a blank flash drive? Or just the original one. I can make you another copy of that one if you want. It might be enough to get Roy out," Sydney suggested. Oscar had gone downstairs to the gallery where Sydney was working on setting up the show. They were planning in his office. He hoped the two heads theory would work this time.

"These people aren't stupid," Oscar said, "They're sure to have a laptop or something to check the authenticity of it before they release Roy."

"What makes you think they'll release Roy at all? If I were them I'd probably kill you too, once I had the disks. What percentage is there in letting you go? The way I see it the only way Walters can feel secure is if he gets control of all the computer information and eliminates everyone who knew about it. Including you and me." Sydney leaned back in Oscar's attorney chair and put her bare feet on the desk. Oscar paced in front of her.

"I could go to the state police or the sheriff. That would be the responsible thing to do. But I worry that they'll send in some gung-ho shoot'em up swat team, and Roy will end up dead anyway."

"How about the FBI?"

"I'm not sure they would take jurisdiction. Plus, it's a bureaucracy we would have to deal with in a limited amount of time. And I may still have the same problem. I think I have to go and explain the problem to them. They can't shoot me. They need to disappear the evidence."

"Don't be stupid. You show up without the disks and you might as well cut your own throat before they do it for you. And there is such a thing as torture. You wouldn't be able to keep anything from them. No. That's definitely not the answer."

Oscar looked out the door, through the gallery, and saw the Channel Three sound truck outside again.

God damned reporters, he thought.

"I have it!" Oscar slapped the top of the desk. Sydney jumped to her feet.

The strip mall parking lot on County Road 721 was just big enough to accommodate the seven television, radio, and newspaper vehicles. In the vacant lot adjacent to the Quick-Stop party store on the end of the row of brick and block buildings the Channel Ten news helicopter was landing in a cloud of blown-up dust, fast food wrappers, and other debris. Reporters and crew were doing sound and video checks on their equipment, drinking coffee and sodas from paper cups. Some were trying to interview Oscar and Sydney.

There were only fifteen minutes left on Rico's deadline. Oscar was keyed up, on an adrenaline high. He called the milling crowd to attention.

"Listen up! Everybody!" They gathered around, aiming their microphones and video cameras at him. Professional silence took over.

"Okay. We went over this once. Now, it's very important that this go down like I explained." Oscar stood on a parking block to get a little height. "All of you follow my car. We're going in fast. You can begin broadcasting as soon as we reach the shack, which is about two hundred yards down the road I'll turn onto. The helicopter..." He pointed at the pilot who had leaned out his door and now nodded, "...will time his approach to coincide with our arrival and hover overhead."

"How do we know they won't shoot at us?" It was Laurie Small from Channel Three. Oscar recognized her as the investigative reporter who had been tracking Roy's case.

"One of the risks of the profession, I guess," Oscar replied. A laugh went up from the reporters and crew. "But I can't believe they would try to shoot anyone with this many witnesses and have it on national television, radio, and in print. These guys are professionals, probably in it for the money. It's not likely they're going to die for whoever hired them."

"Who do you think hired them?" a young male reporter asked, holding his microphone out to catch the answer. Oscar thought the kid looked like Ron Howard when he played Ritchie Cunningham from the old *Happy Days* television show.

"You can do interviews later. Who has a cell phone?" They all raised their hands.

"I need to borrow one to call the police. I don't want them accusing me of not cooperating, and we need somebody to chase the bad guys down after we go in. Be sure to leave them an escape route into the cane field. Now let's saddle up and get out there." Oscar stepped down, accepted a proffered phone and called in a short, but descriptive message to Detective Willis, refusing to answer questions but advising him of the necessity of a speedy response.

He expected Willis would get in touch with the State Police or the local county sheriff immediately, since Oscar was out of the West Palm city jurisdiction, and it should be only a matter of minutes before a patrol car arrived.

Oscar wasn't sure that his plan would work. It made sense to him right then. If it went wrong, he knew it would be his ass that would have to take the blame, not to mention his and Roy's lives. It seemed the best available option, and now he was committed.

Oscar and Sydney led the way in the Toyota, the turnoff being only five miles down the road. Behind him came two big trucks with satellite dishes mounted on top, three vans marked prominently with the logos of their respective news organizations, and two cars filled with print reporters and photographers.

Tall sugar cane stalks flanked both sides of the road, dense and seemingly impenetrable, their white plumes waving in the slight breeze. The road was aging asphalt with no curb, crumbling into the sand at the edges. The sun reflected off the pavement ahead, distorting the light in the heat waves over the road surface. With his arm out one of the open windows to catch some breeze, the stifling heat and humidity was barely tolerable.

Sydney spotted the boiled peanut shack up ahead, and signaled for his turn. The shack might hold a guard, Oscar thought. All he saw inside the small ramshackle structure of corrugated iron and warped plywood were dark shadows, a rusting fifty-five gallon steel drum perched over a low wood fire, and a squat Indian woman in a yellow sack dress. She stood next to the drum, dipping a soggy spoonful of peanuts into a foam cup and hoping for a big sale from the caravan of cars and trucks.

They turned onto the sand trail next to the shack and accelerated down the lane between the canes in a dust-cloud raising line. The Toyota bottomed out and bounced, lurching and swaying too fast down the narrow rutted trail. The big trucks were too wide for the lane and flattened rows of sugar cane on either side as they careened toward the pole barn.

Oscar heard the helicopter's thud-thud-thud and saw it pass over him as he entered the clearing. The sugar cane walled in the open area that was less than fifty yards wide. The sand trail continued through the clearing. There was a shiny white SUV parked next to a single-story white pole barn. One large overhead door faced them, but was closed. The small entry door next to it was open. Sydney pulled the Toyota into the clearing and out of the way to let the other vehicles pass.

They all saw a heavy set man in a Havana-style shirt tear out the door, firing wildly toward the trucks that were skidding to a stop around the perimeter of the clearing. Havana took one shot up in the air toward the helicopter, then stopped to aim at Oscar's car. Sydney floored it. Two bullets passed through the windshield, and then she was on him with a loud thump. Oscar saw the body fly up over the roof of the car. The car skidded on the soft sand and thin grass as Sydney struggled to stop before crashing sideways into the pole barn.

Rico bolted out the door and disappeared into the cane field, hobbling and firing into the air. The helicopter veered off—getting shot at was not part of the job description.

Oscar jumped from the car, his heart pounding, sweat streaming his face from the intense heat and excitement.

He yelled to the building, "Roy! Are you in there?"

No answer. Was the place was empty? Was Roy already dead?

Oscar burst through the doorway, but had to stop, blinded by the transition from the intense sun to the darkness inside the windowless building. His eyes adjusted slowly. He called out again. No answer. He was knocked aside by a cameraman hurrying behind him. They moved farther inside. Someone opened the big overhead door, flooding the interior with light.

Roy was there, tied up on his side on the dirt floor next to an overturned folding chair, his mouth covered with gray duct tape.

Roy's head was drenched in blood and it had soaked into the sand haloing his skull.

Sydney cut him loose with a dagger she pulled from her boot. Oscar jerked the tape in a quick rip, knowing it would hurt. If he was alive.

He was. His face was swollen from a savage beating. He moaned and opened one eye. "That you, Oscar?"

Oscar couldn't help himself. He fell to his knees in the dirt next to Roy as tears spilled down his face with the cameras rolling.

Sydney paced outside, studying the direction Rico had taken. Odds were good either the rattlesnakes or gators would keep him from getting too far.

Chapter Thirty-five

The medical examiner's office opened at eight-thirty Friday morning. Oscar walked in with the staff, having convinced them that as the defense attorney he had a right to information on the deceased Jack Gamble. Dr. Guenther arrived at nine, and made Oscar wait in his outer office while he got his coffee and donut. No one offered Oscar anything. They didn't want him hanging around waiting for the coffee to cool. The office was cold, damp, and clammy, probably because it was located in the basement of the building. The furniture looked like cast-offs not suitable for the higher visibility county offices upstairs. The desks were the old gray steel with scarred rubber tops. Didn't look like CSI's glass and chrome from television at all.

Oscar was flat worn out after staying up late discussing what he knew with the sheriff's detectives, and giving the promised press conference. He was told several other agencies would have many more questions later. They went easy on him since the news was making him out a hero. By the time Oscar hit the bed, Rico had still not been captured. The cane field led off into thousands of acres of jungly field and swamp crawling in poisonous snakes, wild hogs, and alligators. He might never be seen again. One could hope. Roy was hospitalized but just a day or two for observation. He had some cracked ribs, a split lip, broken nose, and a lot of bruising, but no serious injuries. Oscar kidded him that the beating actually improved his looks.

Guenther's desk was orderly, with every item on it arranged in a precise pattern. But based on Guenther's personal appearance, Oscar guessed someone else in the office kept his desk straight.

Guenther was a greasy little middle-aged man with thin black hair he kept in a Donald Trump swoop over his bald spot. The sport coat he wore was a different plaid than the pants, and both were in need of pressing. He was overweight and smelled of cigarette smoke.

It always amazed Oscar to see a doctor smoke, since they, better than anyone, knew the consequences. Guenther had a young male clerk pull the Jack Gamble file for him. Oscar was sitting in the single chair next to the desk. He saw next to him a folder with the name "Willis" written in red ink on it, probably the dental x-rays provided to Detective Willis by the oral surgeon. Guenther fussed with his coffee and donut until the file came in, not even making small talk.

"So," he said as the file was handed to him, "we shall see what we shall see."

He searched through the file, found the appropriate x-rays, and took them along with those from the Willis' file to a light screen on the wall, clipped them onto it and flipped a switch, illuminating the film. Oscar got up and stood next to him, trying to figure out the images.

"They're not the same." Oscar put his index finger on the film to point at the row of teeth in the top film.

"Of course they aren't." Guenther squinted at him as if examining an unusual insect, then turned back to the film. Oscar leaned back a little. Guenther's personal space smelled of cigarettes, garlic, coffee and donuts.

"Even you can see that. If these are indeed the true x-rays of Jack Gamble, then the dead man is someone else. Note the crowns? Mr. Gamble had five nicely made crowns and root canals. The deceased has no crowns, a missing molar, and several fillings. No," he said as he flipped off the light and pulled the film out.

"What about the DNA?" Oscar asked.

"Well, the DNA…" Guenther went back to the file and sorted through it, "…was based on a hair sample. That's enough if it was the right hair. Mr. Gamble had no living relatives so we couldn't type him that way, so the hair that was known to be his was matched to the DNA of the body. We didn't make mistakes. We followed procedure."

"And what if it was somebody else's hair?"

"Then the deceased is definitely not Jack Gamble."

Oscar had Dr. Guenther telephone Detective Willis before he left. This might effectively resolve the murder case against Roy. He couldn't have killed Gamble because most likely Gamble was still alive. At least one would think so since the body from the boat didn't have Jack's teeth. But where was Jack? And who was the person who had been killed? Plus who altered the computer records showing Roy as the one who defrauded the insurance companies. Someone was setting up Roy to take the fall for the insurance rip-off. Oscar had to get his hands back on the original flash drives and take them to the State Attorney's office.

Oscar sat in the car in the parking lot of the medical examiner's office looking around the bullet holes in the windshield of the Toyota deciding his next move. First of all, the police were told that Roy was not responsible for the murder of Jack, who was still likely alive somewhere. And they would now be looking for Rico, as well as, he assumed, R.J. Walters, the father and employer, for Roy's kidnapping and beating. He had to pick up the evidence from the mail. Now. He put the car in reverse to back out of the parking space.

The passenger door opened as he took his foot off the brake, and R.J. Walters got in. His nose was swollen and red, but not bandaged.

Oscar looked around quickly to see if anyone else, like Rico, for instance, was lurking nearby. Nope.

"What do you want, Walters?" Oscar had stopped and looked him over carefully. Had he had air conditioning, the window would have been rolled up and the doors locked, and Walters would be standing outside instead of sitting next to him. He still had the gun in the glove box. But it was right in front of Walters.

Walters was unshaven. He had on one of his thousand dollar suits, but it definitely could use a pressing. He had a valise with him which he set on the floor between his feet. The top was open.

"Leopold. You have no idea the trouble you've caused me. Someone has called the State Bar Association. My office is padlocked. I can't even get in. And that's just part of it. They've frozen all my accounts. I believe you can help—yourself as well as me. I've been following you on my own to talk. There may be a way out of this." The Toyota was blocking the driveway, and a car behind them tapped its horn twice.

"Just drive! Pull out and get on the road," Walters said. Oscar couldn't see the man's right hand since it was tucked inside the left side of his jacket, and had to assume he was armed. He finished backing out and pulled forward into traffic.

"It's over, Walters. I just found out Jack's probably alive. That puts me out of the loop as far as I can see. You should deal with him, or better yet, I'd advise getting a good lawyer."

"Shut up. You're going to give me the computer files. Rico complicated this to the point that it's nearly out of control. Now he wants me to help him."

"You've talked to him? How did he get away?"

"The idiot is off the leash. He carjacked somebody and found his way back to town. I don't know where he is, but I've washed my hands of his mess. I can still straighten this out if I can make the computer records all disappear. There will be no evidence of wrongdoing. Then I can deal with Jack Gamble. Just like I can deal with you." He pulled his arm from his jacket and reached inside the valise.

Oscar was in heavy traffic in the center lane. He hoped Walters didn't have the poor sense to shoot him while he was driving. He thought of running the car into a telephone pole. He glanced over. Walters had pulled his hand out of the bag clutching a handful of hundred dollar bills.

Oscar did a double-take, then laughed out loud. Walters reddened.

"What the hell are you laughing at?"

"You. This is so typical. You still think your money can get you out of this. Sorry, pal, it ain't going to work this time."

"We're brother attorneys, Leopold." He grabbed Oscar's arm. Oscar looked at the hand, and Walters let go. "We can work this out so everybody benefits and nobody gets hurt."

"Too late for that. And you're no brother of mine."

Oscar forced his way into the right hand lane, thinking he would pull over and push Walters and his money out into the street.

At that precise moment the Toyota's transmission gave up the ghost. The clutch was completely gone. It had taken too much abuse lately. Oscar gunned the engine and tried shifting into all five gears, but got no propulsion at all. The engine acted as if he was pushing on the gas while the transmission was in neutral. It just raced. The car coasted to a stop. There was a high curb on his right that didn't allow him to pull the car off the road. He shut it off, turned on the emergency flashers, reached over and took the gun out of the glove box, stuck it in his waistband under his shirt, and got out.

"This is your last chance Leopold," Walters yelled out the open window as Oscar opened the hood. "I'm offering you a half million dollars, tax-free. More money than you'll ever see again in one lump sum. Don't be a loser!" Walters got out of the car. Oscar walked away, abandoning the car and the offer. Walters slammed his fist on the roof, causing a break in one of the small bones of his wrist that would later require a cast. He still held the money in that hand and the valise, probably with more money, in the other. This didn't go unnoticed by the occupants of some of the passing cars.

The cars piling up behind the Toyota began honking. Oscar ignored the curses of the drivers and their not-so-friendly hand signals, waited for an opening in the traffic, walked across the street, and found a working pay phone in the entrance to the

Winn-Dixie. Sydney had been telling him to carry his cell telephone for emergencies like this, but he never remembered. Once again she was right. He looked across the street. Walters was gone.

Sydney answered, saying that she had taken her Harley on an errand but was not far from home. Oscar asked her to bring the Mustang over to pick him up. He stood in the sunshine in front of the store and waited next to a disabled veteran in a wheelchair decorated with dozens of small American flags. He had one leg missing and was collecting coin contributions in exchange for small flag-shaped plastic lapel pins. Only three people dropped coins in the cup while Oscar was there. Oscar gave him five bucks when he saw the Mustang pull into the lot twenty minutes later and clipped the little flag onto his shirt.

Chapter Thirty-six

Ahead of her Sydney had watched the scene with R.J. and Oscar as she had followed him in the Mustang and listened to the conversation over the transmitter she had planted under the Toyota's seat. Oscar wouldn't like her following him, but she was nervous with Rico still out there.

When the Toyota crapped out, she pulled into a driveway to see what happened next, close enough to help if need be. Oscar walked away and Walters stood by the side of the road, clutching a briefcase.

She pulled up and offered Walters a ride. He got in.

The police found him later handcuffed to an electric pole behind a 7-Eleven. There was no briefcase.

Chapter Thirty-seven

Sydney arrived to pick Oscar up, bearing a message.

"Lucy called. She wants to see you."

"What does she want?" Oscar braced his hand against the dashboard while Sydney drove. It was a defensive position against her jack-rabbit starts and last-minute panic stops at every light and stop sign. Oscar had the lap belt on but that wasn't much protection against a collision. Ford had not yet started installing shoulder straps or head rests in 1965, when the Mustang was built.

"She said she has information about Jack. She says it's urgent. She wants to meet you."

"I think we already have that information." He told Sydney about the discovery that Jack was still alive.

"And another thing. Did you hear the news this morning?

"No. I was trying to avoid seeing myself on television. What's up?"

"Remember Seacomb? The other lawyer on the computer list of payoffs?"

"Yes?"

"He was run down by a car last night. Hit and run. Is this just a strange coincidence or is somebody eliminating witnesses?"

Oscar thought about it. First Bascomb, now Seacomb. Someone tried to kill Roy and him. Was Walters behind it? Or maybe Jack himself? Or Rico gone rogue against his father's orders?

Walters was no longer there to help Rico, but Rico may still be acting on his orders. The important thing was now to pick up the computer information and get it to the authorities.

"It's almost noon now. The mail should be at the office. Let's wrap this up. Forget Lucy."

Oscar knew that Lucy had the insurance money. Clifford Ames of Atlantic and Gulf Coast Insurance would not be too happy to find out they paid off on a live body; but that's their problem. As far as he was concerned she and Jack could go live happily ever after somewhere else.

"Do you think Lucy and Jack were together on this?" Sydney asked.

"The same scene played out in Apalachicola. They probably killed her former husband for the insurance money, and then used that to set up the office here. And I think that Tim Bascomb was in on it with them. Or she may be totally innocent and Jack is just using her to get the insurance so he can add that to his stash when he leaves town."

"Have you thought about the possibility that they don't want you or anyone else to have the flash drive? Like I said before, the only way out of this might be to get the computer records and anyone who knows about them. They've killed before. You and Roy are the last links. I think you might be putting yourself at risk here. Why not let the police handle it?"

"Of course I thought about it. I'm not as stupid as I look." Sydney didn't laugh. "But they can't possibly know what I did with the information. Besides, why would Jack want it now? He may have other copies himself. If I were him I'd get the hell out of the country as soon as possible, flash drive or not. They have the two and a half million, plus whatever other millions Jack had hidden away. Why go for the computer information and risk getting caught?"

"Unless he doesn't know that he's been found out. I just found out myself from you. He may want it all and thinks he can still have it. If he knows Walters is behind the killing of Roy and the others, Jack may think he needs the flash drive for insurance.

Or for blackmail. If he gets the one Roy found, the only one left out there is the one implicating Roy."

Just then Sydney's cell rang. She could see from the caller ID it was Lucy. She handed the phone to Oscar.

"Lucy, what's up?"

"Did you get my message? I'm at the city marina on the boat. I've heard from Jack. He's not dead. He's coming for the insurance money. I'm afraid of him—what he might do. Please, Oscar, you've got to help me while there's still time."

"Help you with what? Sounds like this is what you were working toward. Get the money and run. Why didn't you call 911? Or just leave?"

"I didn't know anything about him faking his death. He fooled me too. He's planning on using the boat to escape. I think the cash he stole is hidden on board somewhere. I can't find it. If I call the police they'll arrest him and confiscate everything. I deserve my share. There's no one else I can call. I'll give you half. Just help me keep Jack under control while I search the boat. I have a gun. Then I leave him tied up for the police and we disappear."

"Everybody's trying to make me rich. Just leave. The money's not worth it. Your insurance check is worthless. Even if you managed to cash it the insurance company would have it back before you blinked twice."

"The cash is still good. Are you going to let him kill me? I have something else. Tape recordings Jack made of his conversations with the other lawyers that were involved in the insurance deals. They show Roy had nothing to do with any of it. Jack was setting him up and I can prove it if you help me."

"So you knew of this scam all along?"

"Yes. Now I want compensation. Come quickly, I don't know how long he'll be gone."

He told Sydney the gist of the conversation.

"It's a setup." Sydney had pulled into a parking lot, unsure of their destination.

"Possible, but I would hate to see another person killed in this mess if I have some way to prevent it. And this would clear Roy's name as far as the fraud investigation is concerned. Let's go and see if we can get her and the tapes she's talking about out of there before Jack arrives. We can pick up the mail later. We'll call the police on the way to the marina. We're only a couple of blocks away."

"Just in case, why don't we play it safe?" Sydney said and showed Oscar the little black button transmitter that she was clipping inside her collar at the back of her neck. "I don't want to crush your male ego, but I'm better able to rescue her than you. I'm an expert shot, know martial arts, can run faster than you, and if they are both there they will be expecting you, not me. And I've killed bad guys before. It doesn't keep me awake at night. You can stay in the car, guard my back, and listen in, so if I see anything that looks off kilter, I can tell you. If it all goes bad and the cops aren't here yet you can come to the rescue."

Oscar took the transmitter, pulled the little twenty-five automatic from his waistband, and handed it to Sydney. She pulled back the slide to load a round into the chamber, then stuck it in her belt at the small of her back under her blouse.

"Just cover me, and don't try to help unless it sounds like I need it. I doubt she's going to give me any trouble. The only problem is Jack, and I'll deal with him."

Chapter Thirty-eight

Oscar parked in the marina lot facing the aging Hatteras yacht that sat at the end of the widest part of the dock. Oscar could see the boat from the car. He didn't see Lucy on deck. Sea gulls sat on the bow rail, framed by the water and Palm Beach Island in the distance under the cloudless blue sky.

Sydney talked and tapped the microphone while Oscar listened to be sure it worked.

He couldn't hear the sirens of approaching police cars yet, but he had just made the call.

The marina seemed deserted. The sport fishing boats were unoccupied, waiting for another weekend while their owners attended to their day jobs. A sloop went by under power out in the turquoise water of Lake Worth, probably heading for the inlet to put out to sea. Sydney walked as fast as she could without drawing attention, looking at the other boats as she went by as if searching for someone.

She stepped on board the Hatteras at the stern. The huge boat rocked hardly at all, not reacting to her weight. She smelled the strong odor of gasoline coming from somewhere nearby.

"Lucy!" She called out, not too loudly, "Are you here?"

She looked below, down the companionway.

The square black barrel of an old Army issue .45 just like hers was pointed directly at her nose. She knew it would literally blow her head off at this range.

"Back off."

Sydney backed away.

It was Big Jack. He looked just like he did in his television ads, except he was right side up.

He squeezed his big body up the narrow stairs, keeping the gun directed at her face. He was dressed like a giant weekend sailor with white pants, blue blazer, and a commodore's white cap with gold trim. He had grown a short beard, but it was a feeble attempt at disguise. It was hard to mistake his bulk. Sydney automatically raised her arms halfway on seeing the gun. Lucy followed him up the stairs. Her face was mottled and her eyes swollen as if she had been crying.

"You look pretty healthy for somebody dead, Jack." Sydney hoped Oscar was getting this.

"Shut up. Give me the computer data and we're out of here. Where's the package?"

"I don't have it. It's at the office. I came to pick up Lucy. You aren't going to gain anything by killing us."

"On the contrary, once I have all the evidence and there are no witnesses to testify then I have gained quite a lot. I think you should get below."

Sydney was keenly aware of the smell of gasoline mixed with the fresh fish smell of the salt water. The cries of gulls wheeling overhead seemed unusually loud. It was as if the adrenaline surge of fear had heightened her senses.

"I don't believe I can trust you to stay quiet until we get out of the country. We may yet have time to get to safety if you aren't around," Jack said.

"Who did you kill when you blew up your boat?" Sydney was stalling, trying to give Oscar a chance to help or get help. Where were the police?

"A nobody. A former client who was giving me trouble. He was my size. Two birds with one stone, you might say. Having Lucy identify the body was a nice touch, I thought."

"Billy Grubbs," Sydney guessed.

"That's right. Get below." He gestured again with his gun, trying to herd her down into the gas filled cabin.

"How did you arrange the forensics? The police said the hair samples matched up." Sydney snapped her fingers in a Eureka! "I got it! You pulled some of the poor bastard's hair out before you blew him up, right?"

"I planted the guy's hair in Jack's hairbrush for the police to find," Lucy said.

"What about the dental records? Did you burn down the dentist's office as part of your plan?"

"You're stalling again, but in fact the fire at the dentist's was just coincidence. It gave me the idea to stage my death. Get out of town with some extra cash. Anyway," he pointed with the gun toward the companionway stairs, "enough of this. I'm not here to tell you my life's story. Let's get this over with. Get down the stairs."

"The police know you're not dead." Sydney didn't move, knowing this information would interest him. Could she talk long enough for the police to arrive? From the smell of the fumes coming from Jack and from down below she knew Jack had dumped gasoline in the cabin. The gas would go up like dynamite. Getting below was the last thing she intended to do. Let him shoot her right here. In the open air it was unlikely the fumes would ignite from a muzzle flash. And he might not be familiar with the big gun. It was difficult to shoot it accurately without training, especially with one hand.

"What do you mean?" Jack asked. He had the gun pointed at her belly and her arms were beginning to tire.

"Do you mind if I put my arms down?" She dropped them anyway. She had seen too many movies as a kid. Everybody reached for the sky when confronted with a gun.

"Your dentist. It turns out there was a second set of x-rays at the oral surgeon you went to. They found out today that you're alive. Now they'll be looking for you. I suggest you get all your money out of town quickly. You might not be free long enough to spend much of it."

"You won't be around to know," Jack said.

"Let me guess," Sydney said. "I'm going to die in a boat explosion."

"That's it. It's getting almost boring but still seems effective. I have enough gas in the hold to blow her over the lake and onto the Palm Beach golf course. The bank will be happy when the insurance pays off the note on this tub."

"Jack and I will be out of the country before they know which direction we went. We have a plane chartered. Right, Jack? You're still taking me, right?" Lucy pulled away from Sydney.

"I think this is going to be a solo trip, now that I have the insurance check." He moved the gun to her, then back at Sydney.

"You bastard!" Lucy lunged at Jack, knocking his gun arm aside for a second.

Sydney used the time. She pulled out her own gun and took two quick shots, trying to hit Jack and avoid Lucy. The noise was incredibly loud. Seagulls squealed and took flight nearby. Jack was hit once in the left shoulder. He didn't go down. He shot Lucy in the center of the flamingo picture printed on her blouse. She collapsed on the deck, blood pooling around her. Sydney was ready to shoot again, when both she and Jack heard the airplane-like roar of the big Mustang engine. Jack whipped around to look up the dock.

Oscar had driven over the parking blocks and was now tearing down the narrow wooden dock directly toward the boat, the tires squealing on the wooden planks.

The car was hurtling toward them, fishtailing and picking up speed as it came. Jack emptied his gun, peppering the windshield. Oscar leapt out the door of the speeding car just before Sydney jumped off the side of the boat into the water feet-first and arms wind-milling. The warm water felt icy cold on impact compared to the hot air. She was still going down when she felt, through the water, the impact of the car crashing into the boat, then another heavier thump and a flash of light. She touched the soft bottom with her feet then swam under the surface as far as she could, her lungs aching, trying desperately not to inhale water, then came up forty yards away, gasping for air, tasting the saltwater.

The boat was in flames, burning gasoline flickered on the water nearby, the sound of the fire was a shuddering roar and in the background the sirens were getting louder. The front of the Mustang was imbedded in the hull, having crashed through the side of the boat. The rear bumper held the car balanced precariously on the dock, ready to fall in the water.

She didn't see Oscar.

But she couldn't avoid seeing Jack trying to stand on the moving deck, stumbling, then falling into the wreckage, flames from the gasoline consuming his hair, his clothes, and his body, an image that would stay with her for a lifetime.

Chapter Thirty-nine

The Casa de Lupe Restaurante was in a rundown section of Riviera Beach, just north of West Palm. There was an outdoor patio area with a few rotting picnic tables in the back.

Sydney stood inside the door, letting her eyes adjust to the near darkness of the interior. The place stunk of stale fish grease, cigarettes, and urine. She had parked her motorcycle near the back door of the adjacent building, facing out toward the street.

As her sun-blindness faded, she could see the bar running the length of the room on the left side; no bar stools, only a steel pipe foot rail on the floor along the bar and twenty or so wooden tables with an assortment of mismatched chairs. An exit sign lit up the rear. The only other illumination came from the light behind the bar and three low-wattage bare bulbs hanging by their wires from the ceiling over the table area and over the small coin-operated pool table. Salsa music came from the kitchen.

She stepped up to the bar and ordered a draft beer in Spanish from the Cuban bartender. The other half-dozen patrons were male, gang types, Latino and Anglo. No one gave Sydney any particular notice. She was dressed to look like a man in jeans, boots, and a leather motorcycle jacket. She wore the helmet. She slid a folded fifty-dollar bill across the bar, asking the bartender quietly in Spanish if he had seen Carlos Sanchez.

The bill disappeared quickly, and the bartender nodded toward two men standing at the opposite end of the bar. One had his leg wrapped in a cast. A single crutch was leaning against the end of the bar.

She dragged her beer along the bar top as she approached them, speaking in Spanish.

"What's up? Let me buy a round for you guys. Maybe take the drinks out back and party. I got something for you and need to talk to you about your futures. You won't be sorry, I promise." She removed her helmet, sat it on the bar and shook the long blond hair of her wig loose as she smiled at them.

Sanchez and his friend looked at each other, bumped fists, picked up their beers and followed her out the rear door. A very convincing talk with them at the point of a gun and two hundred fifty thousand in cash was enough to get their agreement to an immediate and permanent return home to Honduras.

Chapter Forty

The police hadn't found Rico yet, but Sydney had, not having to worry about search warrants. She updated her earlier background check on him and dug deeper. She had his home address, another for a condo in Dania Beach, and information on an offshore cigarette boat. Hacking into his computer and credit card records revealed regular monthly payments to a marina in Boca, presumably for dockage fees, then a recent larger payment to the same place.

Rico wasn't at the marina when she checked. The mechanic who worked on the boat hadn't seen him either, saying the instructions had come by telephone. The work was for a rebuild of the boat engine that had blown a head gasket when he tried to take it out a few days ago. The mechanic was annoyed that he was being pressured to do the job ahead of everything else he had to do but said Rico had promised him a bonus for getting the job done quickly.

Sydney assumed Rico was seeing the boat as a safe way out of town. The police would be watching airports, bus stations, and highways. He wasn't at his listed address in Fort Lauderdale and was no doubt trying to get in the wind before the police caught up. So it must be the Dania Beach property. Guys like him sometimes kept a separate discreet place to meet their girlfriends. So it was stake-out the boat or the condo. She decided the condo. He had to be living somewhere, and the boat was not a live-aboard.

His email records showed lots of messages to a woman—not his wife—named Carmen. Probably his current bimbo. She actually had a Facebook page, though it didn't mention Rico. Sydney thought she could pass for Carmen in a quick look if her disguise was good.

A call to a real estate sales office advertising another condo in the same building confirmed that there were no security cameras on site yet, but that it was a very safe building and she shouldn't worry. And it was quiet since most of the owners were absentee and only here for the season.

She watched the entrance carefully from the parking lot for three hours before finally getting lucky and seeing Rico arrive. He had shaved his head and was wearing sunglasses, but she recognized the way he walked and his size. She imagined the police would find him the same way she had sooner or later, but no sign of them now. This had to be quick, before his boat was ready and he escaped. Roy deserved as much. Rico would always be a threat if he weren't stopped now. Even if the police caught Rico first and jailed him, Sydney would never feel that she and Oscar were safe.

It was an ocean-view condo, fifth floor. There was a doorman, actually just a deskman in the lobby where you were supposed to check in. She had dressed in a short slut skirt, with the blond wig similar to Carmen's hair, high heels, a stretch pink tube top, and big sunglasses. While she rarely carried a purse, this time it was handy for concealing bulky items.

The desk clerk let her up after she swished in and leaned over the counter, touched his arm and announced breathlessly that she was expected by Mr. Richard Walters, but she was a little late. Would he mind calling up to let him know Carmen had just arrived? He had her sign the register and she kept the pen, went on to the elevators, put on black rubber surgical gloves, and punched the button for floor five. She tapped softly on the door of suite 510 with the butt of the automatic, then held it behind her back and turned her head to the side. The peephole darkened, and he fumbled with the lock and opened the door, expecting anyone but her. He started to speak, then realized she was not Carmen. He had a gun in his hand, but Sydney had the element of surprise and the quickness of experience and youth.

Two shots to his head and one to the heart. He fell back into the room with a thud. Blood and brains spattered the adjacent door to the bathroom. The smell of cordite and open flesh caused her nostrils to flare. She picked up the spent brass and unscrewed the silencer, putting it under the false bottom of her bag, then quickly broke down the gun, removed the barrel and kept that too, leaving the gun frame. The police would be frustrated and confused with that one. Let them waste some time investigating a dead end. But she didn't want to get caught carrying the gun out nor leave anything for ballistics. Most people wouldn't recognize the barrel and silencer for what they were, and in any event, these would soon be dumped and not likely turned in even if they were found. She waited a moment for any sound of others on the floor, heard nothing, pulled off the wig and from her bag removed a plus-size silk scarf. She wrapped it around her shoulders and waist, turning it into a blue dress. then closed the door softly. She left via the stairs, where the emergency door led directly into the parking lot.

Chapter Forty-one

"The People of the State of Florida versus Oscar Leopold, case number 713543," the clerk announced.

"Are the people ready to proceed?" the judge asked, looking inquisitively over the open file in front of him at Sheila. Roy and Oscar sat at the defense table farthest from the jury box.

"Your honor, the people respectfully request an adjournment of this case. We've been unable to locate our complaining witness, Mr. Sanchez, and the other witnesses. I am sure that if we can have a few days adjournment we'll have them in court." Sheila shuffled her papers and looked hopefully back to the courtroom door for anyone.

Roy stood.

"Your honor, I am here with my client as scheduled and ready to go ahead to trial. A jury has been brought in. Everyone is ready, it seems, but the state. I ask that in the interest of justice the case be dismissed with prejudice."

Sheila jumped to her feet.

"Your honor! I object to any dismissal of the very serious charges here. I am sure that if we can have a few days we can locate Mr. Sanchez and have him and the others here to testify. The detectives talked to him just the other day, and he was subpoenaed and planning on being present. I am sure there's a good reason why he was unable to appear.

"Sit down, Ms. Katz. This trial has been scheduled for several weeks now, and you and Mr. Sanchez have had plenty of opportunity to clear your calendars for the proceedings. And where are your other witnesses? I cannot imagine what could be more important to you all than my time."

Oscar smiled.

The judge made some notes in the file and handed it to the bailiff.

"So ordered. The charges are dismissed with prejudice. And next time, Ms. Katz, I suggest that you be ready and not waste the time of this court."

Oscar blew Sheila a kiss as he and Roy walked out.

Chapter Forty-two

Openings at the Rose Madder gallery were supposed to end at nine, but Oscar left the doors open as long as the artist and visitors wanted to be there. This had been a big one, with roughly two hundred people. Most of the crowd consisted of other artists, Oscar's friends, and those from the neighborhood who wanted the free wine and appetizers.

Sydney was the most exotic one there, dressed in soft black leather pants, thigh-high black boots, and an unbuttoned short black leather jacket with nothing underneath. Her black lipstick and fingernails matched the outfit. More women than men hit on her, which didn't surprise her.

By eleven everyone was gone, leaving Sydney and Oscar to survey the mess left behind. Plastic wine glasses, paper plates, and napkins lay on window ledges, along the floor near the walls, and overflowed the two wastebaskets.

Sydney locked the door and turned off the main gallery lights. There was still one group on the sidewalk talking. The artist, her husband, and some of her friends had left early for dinner, not inviting Oscar, which he didn't mind. She turned out to be much like her paintings, dark, moody, and forbidding. Not much fun.

The media show had moved on to other attractions, now that Jack was dead for sure this time and Walters was in jail. Oscar no longer had cops, reporters, and lawyers after him. He would have to testify in Walters' trial, but that would be down the road a way and only if he didn't plea-bargain. The way the prosecutors were talking, there would be no deals cut for him and, given his age, he would likely die in jail.

Roy had gotten together with the other associates in Jack's old firm to take over the abandoned files. He continued the advertising, but in a more restrained and dignified form. He made an appearance at the opening and even bought one of the paintings. The most expensive one.

Just before people started arriving, Sydney showed him his present. She took him out the back door. Two nearly identical 1965 Ford Mustang convertibles with the tops down were parked on either side of the Buick.

"Only one of them is yours," she said, pointing to the yellow one. "It has the lowest mileage and is all original. Mine, the candy-apple red one, has a remanufactured high-performance engine, dual carbs, racing suspension, speed shifter, and a custom Alpine sound system. I might let you drive it if you're nice."

"How did you do this? These cost a fortune."

Sydney smiled.

She shrieked as he picked her up by the waist, dropped her into the passenger seat, and they went for the first test drive.

Author's Note

Anyone who has lived in Florida may recognize that I have taken liberties with street names, invented some locations, and taken liberties with the descriptions of others. The characters are of course entirely fictional, and none of the events have taken place, so far as I know.

Boats don't explode nearly as often as I suggest.

To receive a free catalog of Poisoned Pen Press titles, please contact us in one of the following ways:

Phone: 1-800-421-3976
Facsimile: 1-480-949-1707
Email: info@poisonedpenpress.com
Website: www.poisonedpenpress.com

Poisoned Pen Press
6962 E. First Ave. Ste 103
Scottsdale, AZ 85251